THE FIRST DAY

"Hey, guys, come here," Jana called at last. "I think I've found it." The others hurried over to where she was standing. "This spot is perfect. From here we can see everything that's going on at the front of Wakeman Junior High."

To Jana's relief, the others looked around and then agreed.

"So now we've got our list of critical things to remember and our special spot," said Christie. "I think we should meet somewhere on the first day of school and walk together."

"Do you mean meet somewhere away from school so we can get our act together before we face junior high?" asked Jana.

Christie nodded. "I was thinking about the corner by Nugent's grocery around eight-thirty."

"Great," said Melanie. "We'll come straight to this spot and wait for the bell. It will be just the same as Mark Twain Elementary."

The others nodded.

"Well, Fabulous Five," said Katie. "I think we're ready."

"As ready as we'll ever be," said Jana. But later, when she thought back on it, she realized that they hadn't been ready for junior high at all. . . .

Bantam Skylark Books by Betsy Haynes
Ask your bookseller for the books you have missed

THE AGAINST TAFFY SINCLAIR CLUB
TAFFY SINCLAIR STRIKES AGAIN
TAFFY SINCLAIR, QUEEN OF THE SOAPS
TAFFY SINCLAIR AND THE ROMANCE
MACHINE DISASTER
BLACKMAILED BY TAFFY SINCLAIR
TAFFY SINCLAIR, BABY ASHLEY,
AND ME
THE GREAT MOM SWAP
THE GREAT BOYFRIEND TRAP

Books in The Fabulous Five Series:
#1 SEVENTH-GRADE RUMORS

THE FABULOUS FIVE

Seventh-Grade Rumors

BETSY HAYNES

BANTAM BOOKS
NEW YORK • TORONTO • LONDON • SYDNEY • AUCKLAND

RL 5, 009–012

SEVENTH-GRADE RUMORS
A Bantam Skylark Book / September 1988

Skylark Books is a registered trademark of Bantam Books, a division of Bantam Doubleday Dell Publishing Group, Inc. Registered in U.S. Patent and Trademark Office and elsewhere.

ISBN 0-553-15625-X

Published simultaneously in the United States and Canada

Bantam Books are published by Bantam Books, a division of Bantam Doubleday Dell Publishing Group, Inc. Its trademark, consisting of the words "Bantam Books" and the portrayal of a rooster, is Registered in U.S. Patent and Trademark Office and in other countries. Marca Registrada. Bantam Books, 666 Fifth Avenue, New York, New York 10103.

PRINTED IN THE UNITED STATES OF AMERICA

0 9 8 7 6

CW

Seventh-Grade
Rumors

CHAPTER 1

"Come on, Melanie. An iguana is a lizard. I mean, we're talking MAJOR lizard here. Not your standard garden variety, and I'm telling you, nobody has one of those things for a pet," said Katie Shannon, rolling her eyes heavenward to show her disbelief.

Melanie Edwards was unperturbed. "Shane Arrington does," she insisted. "At least that's what I hear. They say his parents are hippies, and that he has a pet iguana named Igor."

"Big deal," said Christie Winchell. "Did you hear about Jon Smith?"

"What a boring name," sniffed Melanie.

"His name may be boring, but his parents aren't. They're celebrities!" said Christie in a rush of excitement. "You know who they are. Chip Smith, the sports director on the local television station. Mrs. Smith goes by the name Marge Whitworth. She's the news anchorwoman who also has her own afternoon talk show that's juicier than *The Oprah Winfrey Show.*"

"Wow! I know her," shouted Jana Morgan. "She's the one who interviewed Taffy Sinclair and me on TV when we found baby Ashley. I didn't know she had a *son*!"

"Can't you talk about anything but boys?" Katie asked sourly. "I don't suppose any of you have heard about Whitney Larkin? She has this mega-high IQ, somewhere around a zillion, and she's *supposed* to be in *sixth* grade this year, not seventh. She's skipping a grade because she's so brilliant. Can you imagine what it would be like to have *her* in one of your classes?"

"That's nothing. Wait until you hear this!" Beth Barry butted in. "Laura McCall is this really big deal girl from Riverfield Elementary and *I heard* that she's as pretty as Taffy Sinclair and maybe even prettier. But that's not all. Get this. She has all the girls from her school eating out of her hand because her parents are divorced and she lives with her father, who is hardly ever home, and she can do *anything she wants*. What I hear is"—Beth paused for dramatic effect—"going to her house is a real blast."

"Great." Jana groaned, giving her favorite stuffed bear a big hug. It was Labor Day weekend, the last

Saturday before school started, and she and her four best friends would enter Wakeman Junior High, or Wacko Junior High, as most kids called it. The girls were having a regular meeting of their self-improvement club, The Fabulous Five, in Jana's bedroom. Today the conversation kept drifting away from self-improvement and toward rumors they had heard about the kids from Riverfield and Copper Beach Elementary schools whom they would be meeting for the first time on Tuesday morning.

The five friends had stuck together through thick and thin, weathered every grade school crisis together, especially when that crisis involved their arch-rival, Taffy Sinclair. Beautiful, snooty Taffy, who did everything she could to make life miserable for The Fabulous Five.

"I heard a rumor about Laura McCall, too," Melanie was saying. "I heard that she and her friends have a club called The Fantastic Foursome and that Laura is the leader. What I heard is that to stay in the club, you have to do whatever Laura tells you to do. If you won't do it, you're out!"

"Wow," said Jana. "What does she make them do?"

Melanie shrugged. "I don't know. I couldn't find out any more."

"This probably sounds weird," said Christie, "but sometimes I wish we were going back to Mark Twain Elementary this year instead of on to junior high. I mean, we had things under control there. Everybody knew us. Things like that."

"Right," said Melanie. "I know just how you feel. I'm tired of being treated like a baby, especially by my parents, but I'm not sure I'm ready for junior high. To be perfectly honest, I don't feel that much older than I did when school was out in June."

Beth scowled. "Get serious, Edwards. Of course you're older. We all are."

"Hey, do you think we *look* older?" asked Jana. She jumped to her feet and swung open the closet door where her full-length mirror hung. Giggles erupted behind her as her friends crowded forward to strike poses and peer at their reflections.

Jana stepped aside and looked at the others. Beth had been her best friend practically forever. They had started kindergarten together, and Jana had liked her bright personality instantly. Beth the clown, Jana thought with a smile, remembering how her dark-haired friend had kept everyone in stitches with her antics. She hadn't changed much either, except that now, instead of a clown, she was a dramatic actress, grabbing attention with her wild clothes and her theatrical flourishes.

Naturally, Christie Winchell had been in that kindergarten class, too, since her mother was principal of the school. Taller than any of the others, thin, blond, and athletic, Christie was the smart one of the group, practically a mathematical genius, but she was also a super friend—quiet but caring.

Melanie Edwards, who had moved to their town in second grade, was in love with love. That figured since everything about her was romantic, from her huge blue eyes to her soft reddish-brown hair that lay in wispy curls around her face, and especially her attitude about boys. She was also a little gullible, believing practically anything, which made it fun sometimes to tell her something bizarre.

In all the years they had been friends, thought Jana, Katie Shannon was the only one who had really changed. She had been a shy little red-haired girl when she entered Mark Twain Elementary in third grade. But then in fourth, her mother had become active in the women's movement, and Katie had blossomed into a pint-size feminist, announcing her views loudly to anyone who would listen.

"I'll bet we look just as old as Laura McCall and her friends." Melanie swept her hair on top of her head and tilted her chin. "They may think that they're big deals, but we'll show *them*. Look out for The Fabulous Five, Laura McCall!"

Everyone laughed.

"The thing I'm worried about is that Wakeman is so huge," said Christie. "We won't know half the kids."

"Or where our classes are," added Katie.

"Or where the girls' bathrooms are!" Beth said, giggling.

"What that really means is that we have to stick together even more than before." Jana knew she sounded more confident than she felt. "We can't let anyone know how nervous we are, and we definitely can't let those other kids run over us."

Christie frowned. "Don't forget. To them, we're the *other* kids."

"Okay, gang. Let's get organized," said Katie. "When we hit Wacko Junior High on Tuesday morning, we're going to do it with a unified front."

Jana tried to swallow a giggle. Katie's front was as flat as a pancake. "What did you have in mind?" she asked with a grin.

"To start with, we need to make a list of all the essential things to remember," said Katie. "Like the gum tree."

"Right!" said Melanie. "We can't forget that."

Jana opened a brand-new spiral notebook lying on her desk and wrote "1. Gum Tree" on the first page. The gum tree was important. Mr. Bell, the Wakeman principal, was an absolute fanatic when it came to the way he hated chewing gum, and the students had selected the oak tree beside the front door and dubbed it the gum tree a few years before. Ever since then, every morning when the first bell rang, all the kids who were chewing gum stuck it to the tree before going in. Even Mr. Bell had liked the idea, and it had become a school tradition.

"Put this down on the list," instructed Melanie. "Never, NEVER ask a ninth-grader for directions to a classroom. My cousin Darcy did that last year. She ended up at the opposite end of the building standing outside the boys' bathroom. By the time she found the right room, she was ten minutes late to class."

"And I can't forget to put down the movie on Friday night and going to Bumpers afterwards," Jana added, writing as fast as she could. Bumpers was a fast food restaurant that was also the exclusive hangout of the kids from Wakeman Junior High after school and on Friday nights. She could hardly wait to go there.

"I'm even going to miss Mama Mia's Pizzeria." Christie sighed. "We had a lot of good times there."

Jana felt a little sad when she thought about not going to Mama Mia's anymore. She and Randy Kirwan had had their first date there, and he had kissed her later. She felt dreamy when she thought about him. She hoped he would still be her boyfriend at Wakeman Junior High.

Nobody could think of anything else to put on the list. "I'm still nervous," said Jana as she made copies for everybody on sheets of notebook paper. "I mean, we're so *used* to Mark Twain Elementary, and everybody there was used to us. The other kids looked up to us because we were the oldest. We even had our own spot by the fence where we could talk privately. Everybody knew it was our spot and nobody bothered us."

Beth jumped to her feet. "Wow! What a COLOSSAL idea! Morgan, you're a genius."

"What are you talking about?" Jana asked.

"Come on, guys," said Beth. "Let's go over to Wakeman right now. There won't be anybody there on Saturday afternoon, so we can pick out our own private spot by the Wakeman fence. Don't you get it? It will be just like Mark Twain Elementary."

The girls scrambled out of Jana's apartment and hurried the six blocks to the junior high. It was a sprawling, rectangular, single-story building with a courtyard in the center resembling a squared-off donut, and it was made of cream-colored brick. The school ground was surrounded by a chain link fence, just as Mark Twain Elementary had been, with a sign at the front proudly proclaiming it to be "Wakeman Junior High, Home of the Wakeman Warriors." Beth had been right about the place's being deserted, and soon the five of them were darting from one end of the fence to the other looking for the perfect spot.

"Hey, guys, come here," Jana called at last. "I think I've found it." The place Jana referred to was in the front left corner of the grounds. "This is perfect," she said as the others hurried to her. "We can see everything that's going on at the front of the school and also anybody who's heading this way from two different directions or getting off the buses."

To Jana's relief, the others looked around and then agreed.

"So now we've got our list of critical things to remember and our special spot by the fence," said

Christie. "I think we should meet somewhere on Tuesday morning and walk to school together. You know, with a unified front, like Katie said."

"Do you mean meet somewhere away from school where nobody will see us so we can get our act together before we face junior high?" asked Jana.

Christie nodded. "I was thinking about the corner by Nugent's grocery around eight-thirty."

"Great," said Melanie. "We'll come straight to this spot and wait for the bell. It will be just the same as Mark Twain Elementary."

The others nodded.

"Well, Fabulous Five," said Katie. "I think we're ready."

"As ready as we'll ever be," said Jana. But later, when she thought back on it, she realized that they hadn't been ready for junior high at all.

CHAPTER

"Oh, my gosh!" shrieked Beth. "*Look!* They're standing in our spot!"

Jana and her friends had just entered the gates of Wakeman Junior High on Tuesday morning and were making their way across the crowded school ground toward the front left corner of the fence, just as they had planned. At Beth's outburst they stopped in their tracks and looked with surprise in the direction she was pointing.

"Oh, no!" cried Jana. It was true. Four girls were standing in the very spot that The Fabulous Five had picked for their own on Saturday, looking as if the world belonged to them. One was a tall blonde whose hair had been caught on top of her head and fell over one shoulder in a braid that came almost to her waist. Beside her stood her exact opposite, a small dark-haired girl who had a short haircut and enormous brown eyes. Next to her was another blonde, and finally stood a wide-eyed brunette with long, wavy hair. It was obvious who was in control—the tall blonde with the waist-length braid. The moment she spoke the other three turned toward her with the precision of a drill team and seemed to hang on every word.

"Laura McCall," Melanie muttered. "I know it's her. It has to be."

"What are *they* doing in our place?" Beth demanded. "Come on. Let's get them out of there."

"How?" asked Christie. "This is a public school. They have as much right to be there as we do."

Beth didn't seem to hear. She was heading straight toward the other girls with a look of grim determination on her face.

"Beth!" insisted Jana, running after her best friend. The others hurried after her. When Jana caught up to Beth less than ten feet from where the others stood, she grabbed her by the arm. "Wait. We can't just go barreling up to them and tell them to get out of our private spot. After all, Christie's right. This is a public school."

"Whatever we do, we have to stick together," said Melanie.

"Yeah," said Katie. "Remember that we're The Fabulous Five." Then she paused, throwing an angry look toward Laura McCall and her followers. "The Fantastic Foursome," she scoffed. "Big deal."

By now it was obvious to Jana that The Fantastic Foursome had noticed The Fabulous Five. They were gazing at them with scorn.

"I don't like this," said Melanie in a voice that was almost a whimper. "Let's get out of here."

"Don't be ridiculous," barked Beth. "They're not going to scare me off."

Katie moved up to stand beside Beth. "Me either," she said.

At the same instant, Laura McCall stepped forward. "What do you want?" she challenged.

"Did you *lose* something?" asked the short dark-haired girl beside her.

"Of course not," Beth threw back at her. "We just wanted to look you over since we've heard so much about you."

Laura McCall froze instantly. Her eyes hardened as she looked straight at Beth. "You'd better watch it!" She spat out the words menacingly, and before Beth could respond, the other blonde chimed in, "You must be Beth Barry. WE can TELL."

The three girls standing beside Laura giggled among themselves. "You're the show-off," Laura assured her.

Jana felt a burst of anger at Laura for saying such a thing. Beth was dressed in chartreuse stirrup pants and a chartreuse and electric-pink shirt that hung past her knees. It was funny how you stopped really looking at someone you knew so well, thought Jana. You stopped noticing things that were pretty obvious to everyone else, such as Beth's wild taste in clothes. But that didn't make her a show-off. She was just a little theatrical, that was all. Jana opened her mouth to come to her friend's defense, but Beth was ready with a challenge of her own.

"What do you mean by that?" she said.

"Figure it out," said Laura. Then she turned abruptly and strode off in the direction of the school with the other three marching along behind.

"Hey, don't pay any attention to them. It's all sour grapes. Besides, we've got our spot back," called Katie as she rushed toward the corner of the fence. "Way to go, Beth!"

Beth didn't answer. She was looking angrily over her shoulder at Laura McCall and her friends.

"They think they know everything," Christie mumbled. "Boy, are they in for a surprise."

Everybody nodded and eagerly followed Katie to the fence. All except Jana. She ambled after the others, but her thoughts were on her best friend again. She couldn't get over Beth's strange behavior. Jana frowned. Beth was always loud and dramatic, but she never purposely picked a fight. Especially with someone she didn't know and certainly had no quarrel with. That just wasn't like her. She must really be nervous about junior high, thought Jana. Beth was the one who was always laughing and making everyone else relax, but this morning she was totally uptight.

Also, Jana couldn't help wondering if someone was spreading rumors about Beth. If so, maybe those rumors extended to herself and the rest of her friends. After all, Laura hadn't said *you're A show-off.* She had said *you're THE show-off,* as if she had more labels that she was just waiting to slap onto other kids whenever she felt like it. I wonder what my label is? *The* what?

Jana leaned against the fence and tried to relax, but her insides were quivering. In fact, she couldn't remember when she had felt so insecure. Somehow, standing in their special corner now that the others were gone didn't feel the same as it had at Mark Twain Elementary. The sea of unfamiliar faces around her grew larger and larger as it got nearer to time for the bell.

She glanced down at the denim skirt and layered top she was wearing. Even deciding what to wear on the first day of school had been a trauma because first impressions were so important. They affected what people thought of you. Even what labels they stuck on you, she thought with a shudder.

An unexpected heat wave had made the new wool pants outfit she had so carefully picked out for the first day of school out of the question, and her mother had immediately vetoed jeans. Jana had pulled practically everything she owned out of her closet and pitched it onto the bed. Then she had tried on things in one combination after another until she had finally settled on the denim skirt. Still, the moment she had stepped out the front door and knew that it was too late to change again, she panicked. What if she looked weird? What if nobody else in the entire junior high wore a denim skirt today? Or even worse, what if all the *wrong* kids wore them and all the neat kids had on wool pants outfits?

She had felt a little better when she got to the corner by Nugent's and found that Melanie, too, was wearing a denim skirt. At least if she was laughed at, she wouldn't be alone. Now, as she scanned the crowd of kids streaming onto the school ground, her confidence plunged again. Hardly anyone was wearing a denim skirt.

Students were milling around in front of the school and standing in groups talking, but nobody seemed to notice The Fabulous Five or pay any attention to them. It was as if they were invisible.

Christie must have felt it, too. "Maybe we ought to walk around and see if we can find some other kids from Mark Twain Elementary," she suggested. "I don't know about you guys, but I feel sort of out of it standing way over here."

"Me, too," said Jana. "Creepy, as a matter of fact. I just saw Alexis Duvall and Lisa Snow heading toward the other side of the school ground. Maybe we should go over and talk to them."

"I've got a better idea," said Katie. "Let's go in and find our homerooms before the bell rings. That way, hopefully, we won't get lost and have to ask a ninth-grader for directions."

"And maybe we'll see some cute boys," offered Melanie. "I haven't seen Scott yet, and I'm *dying* to get a look at Shane Arrington. Come on, guys. What are we waiting for?"

Everybody liked that idea, especially Jana. She had been watching for Randy Kirwan ever since she got to school. What if they didn't have any classes together this year? She would absolutely die.

The girls walked in the front door and stopped beside the office, checking their schedule cards. The corridors were almost empty. It would be easy to locate their homerooms before the bell rang.

"My homeroom is one oh seven," said Jana.

"So is mine," said Christie, "and according to the sign, it should be down the hall to the left."

Jana and her friends studied the sign that was taped to the outside of the office window. It had an arrow pointing left beside Rooms 100–115 and another arrow pointing right beside Rooms 116–130.

Melanie, Katie, and Beth all had homerooms in the opposite direction. "We'll see you at lunch," called Melanie.

"If we last that long," joked Jana, relieved that seventh-graders had the first of the three lunch periods.

Turning into the left corridor, Jana and Christie hurried along, scanning the first few room numbers. Suddenly Christie stopped short and reached out a hand to halt Jana.

Looking up, Jana saw that five or six boys, probably ninth-graders, were lined up in the hall. They were watching the two approach with amused smiles on their faces.

"Hey, guys, look what we have here," one of them said. "Seventh-grade girls. What do you think?"

"Ignore them and just keep walking," Christie whispered hoarsely. "Act natural."

Jana tried, but her legs felt instantly stiff. Her knees didn't want to bend and her feet shuffled noisily across the floor.

"I'd say they're threes," called a boy from the far end of the line. "Three and a half, tops."

"Naw, three is too generous."

Jana cringed. Suddenly she knew what was going on. The boys were ninth-graders looking over the new crop of seventh-grade girls, and they were stationed along the hallway to rate—probably on a scale of one to ten—any seventh-grade girls unlucky enough to come by.

Three is too generous! she thought angrily. Of all the nerve. But then, who cared what a few ninth-grade boys thought, anyway? The important thing was to get out of there and find the right room before the bell rang.

Suddenly the boys started hooting and clapping. "Ten! Ten!" someone shouted.

Surprised, Jana turned around to see Laura McCall sauntering up the hall with her long blond braid bouncing over her shoulder and a triumphant gleam in her eye.

CHAPTER

Jana and Christie ducked into room 107 and sank into seats near the door. They were the first ones to arrive for homeroom, and they exchanged looks of relief at being out of sight of the ninth-grade boys.

"That was disgusting!" said Christie. "How dare those boys rate us, anyway?"

"And can you imagine rating Laura McCall a *ten*?" Jana huffed.

Gradually other kids drifted into the room and found seats. Most of them looked a little bewildered at the newness of Wakeman and the difference in the school routine. Jana could sympathize. She felt that way herself. She dreaded changing rooms every hour and being stuck in classes without any of her friends.

The first familiar face to come through the door belonged to Curtis Trowbridge. Naturally he would be early for class, thought Jana. Curtis was not only the nerd of the world, he was Mr. Enthusiasm, always raising his hand and always the first one to volunteer—no matter what. He had been the sixth-grade editor for the *Mark Twain Sentinel*, but the worst thing about him, Jana thought, was his lifelong crush on her.

Curtis came tearing into the room as if nothing could start until he got there. Just then the first bell rang, and more kids started pouring into the room and scrambling to find seats.

Jana watched the door for anyone else she knew. Clarence Marshall came in with Matt Zeboski. They had been in her class at Mark Twain Elementary, and Clarence had almost been held back. The only other girls from her school were Taffy Sinclair and Mona Vaughn, who entered the room together. As usual, Taffy looked gorgeous. Her blond hair had grown longer over the summer and deep streaks of eye shadow accented her big blue eyes. Makeup! Jana suppressed the urge to frown. Taffy had been her enemy for ages, but she had also been getting a little bit nicer lately, especially since she lost her diary at the end of school last year and thought for a while that everyone knew her secrets.

Jana was so busy watching Taffy that she almost missed seeing someone else come into her homeroom. A sharp jab in the ribs from Christie brought her to attention.

"Look," Christie whispered. "There's Laura McCall."

Tall, blond Laura flipped her long braid over her shoulder as she stood by the door surveying the room. Beside her were two of the friends who had been standing with her at the fence. One was the small girl with the short, dark hair, and the other was the second blonde.

"Oh, no," groaned Jana as they headed for three seats together on the other side of the room. "Not that bunch."

"That's all we need," whispered Christie. "I have a feeling that they are going to show up just about everywhere we don't want them to be."

Just then the last bell rang, and kids who weren't in seats scrambled to find them, running into each other and creating lots of confusion. While everyone was getting settled, Jana opened her notebook and dug around in her purse for a pencil. Suddenly she was aware that the room had gotten totally silent. Glancing up toward the teacher's desk to see what was going on, she discovered that she was looking straight into the face of her former fifth-grade teacher, Mr. Neal. *Dreamy* Mr. Neal, she had always called him because he was the youngest and most handsome teacher she had ever seen. Standing behind his desk and gazing out at the class, he looked as dreamy as ever in his dark, tweed jacket with the leather patches on the elbows. Her heart began to pound and she could feel her ears getting hot.

Jana chanced a quick look at Christie, who was looking back sympathetically. Christie knew that Jana had had a terrible crush on Mr. Neal in fifth grade, just as she knew about Christie's crush last year on Mr. Scott, the new assistant principal at Mark Twain Elementary. *But what is Mr. Neal doing here at Wakeman Junior High?* she wanted to shout.

"Good morning, students, and welcome to Wakeman," he said in a husky voice. "This will be your homeroom every morning for the first thirty minutes of the school day, and I'll be your homeroom teacher. We'll use this time to conduct business, such as attendance and announcements, so that your other class periods will be free for study."

Someone in the back of the room groaned, causing a few others to giggle. Mr. Neal ignored them and went on.

"My name is Mr. Neal, and we'll begin this morning as every morning by taking attendance."

Jana slowly let out a breath that she wasn't even aware she was holding and sank back in her seat to listen for her name. Mr. Neal, Mr. Neal, Mr. Neal, she repeated over and over again to herself. *Dreamy* Mr. Neal!

"Shane Arrington," she heard Mr. Neal call, and she bolted up in her seat.

"Here," answered an incredibly handsome blond boy near the front. So that's Shane Arrington, Jana mused. The kid with the iguana. Just wait until I tell Melanie that he's in my homeroom.

Now that Shane had caught her attention, Jana listened closely to the names Mr. Neal called. Laura's short, dark-haired friend answered to "Tammy Lucero," and the blonde to "Melissa McConnell." Jana wrote both names in her notebook. But that was not the end of surprises.

"Randy Kirwan," called Mr. Neal.

When Randy answered, Jana followed the sound of his voice and discovered that he had come into the room without her seeing him and was sitting two rows over and one seat back. When she looked at him, he looked at her, too, flashing one of the 1,000-watt smiles that he always saved for her.

Jana returned his smile, feeling a warm glow. Randy Kirwan had dark, wavy hair and blue eyes and was the handsomest and most wonderful boy in the world, and fortunately he was also her boyfriend. He had taken her to Mama Mia's for pizza and to a movie, and he had already kissed her twice. But all of that happened last year when they were sixth-graders at Mark Twain, and she had wondered a hundred times during the summer if things would be different between them in junior high. Now, to her immense relief, she knew that they would not.

Since he was in her homeroom, she couldn't help wondering if he was in any of her other classes, too.

She was reaching for her notebook to write him a note when she was jarred back to reality by the sound of her name.

"Jana Morgan! Is Jana Morgan present?"

Jana jumped to attention. From the tone of Mr. Neal's voice, she knew that wasn't the first time he had called her name.

"Yes, sir. Right here," she answered quickly. She could see out of the corner of her eye that Laura McCall and her two friends were snickering.

Jana looked at her watch, wishing with all her might that homeroom would be over. It was 9:10. Twenty more minutes to go.

Next Mr. Neal passed out Student Handbooks, instructing the class to put their names on the covers, not to lose them, and to pay particular attention to the school dress code on page 4.

"These are the rules you'll all live by for the next three years," he said with a faint smile.

Jana skimmed the list of dress code rules. 1. Boys' and girls' hair should be kept clean, neat, and well-groomed—blah, blah, blah, not cause a health or safety hazard, blah, blah, blah. 2. Girls are expected to wear clothing in keeping with their gender—blah, blah, blah. 3. Boys are expected to wear clothing in keeping with their gender. Jana paused and giggled to herself at the vision of Randy showing up for school dressed like a girl. 4. Students are not to wear T-shirts with logos, pictures, phrases, letters, or words on them that are obscene or disruptive. . . .

"Now that you've absorbed the rules, turn to page twenty-eight," Mr. Neal said, interrupting Jana's reading. He was smiling, and Jana started smiling, too, when she saw that on page 28 was what she had been waiting for, the list of student activities.

She felt a shiver of excitement as she ran her finger down the names of the clubs and activities, many of them available for the very first time in junior high. Cheerleading. Yearbook. School newspaper. Drama club. Band. Football. Basketball. Soccer. The list was practically endless. And beside each activity was the date next week of the sign-up meeting or tryouts.

All over the room kids were talking eagerly to each other, and Christie leaned across the aisle and said, "Gosh, Jana. There are so *many*. I don't know what to sign up for. What about you?"

"I don't know either," Jana confessed. "I want to do almost everything. Yearbook. School newspaper. Maybe even cheerleading."

"I'm thinking about going out for girls' basketball," said Christie. "And maybe yearbook."

"Will you try out for cheerleader if I do?" Jana asked. "I'm dying to do it, but I don't want to do it alone."

Before Christie could answer, Jana jerked her head around. She had the crazy feeling that someone was looking at her. She was right. Laura McCall and her two friends were whispering together and looking straight at Jana and Christie. "Get a load of those three," Jana said, nudging Christie and nodding in their direction. "What do you think they're talking about?"

"Us, of course," said Christie. "They're probably reading our lips to try to find out which activities we're going out for so that they can go out for them, too. I have the feeling that they're going to be our biggest competition."

"Me, too," Jana growled. "The Fantastic Foursome!" she added, spitting out the words. "We've got to show them that they can't run over The Fabulous Five!"

CHAPTER

Beth and Katie were already sitting at a table in the crowded cafeteria when Jana sank down beside them. This lunchroom was almost twice the size of the one at Mark Twain, and she had felt a moment of panic until she spotted her friends.

"Whew! I made it," she said with a sigh.

"So how did it go?" asked Katie. "It looks as if you survived your first morning in junior high."

"Barely," said Jana, shaking her head. "This place is wild." She went on to tell Beth and Katie about the lineup of ninth-grade boys in the hallway before class who were rating seventh-grade girls on a scale of one to ten. "It was disgusting. But that was just the beginning. Christie and I got to our homeroom okay, and there were even some kids in there that we knew. Randy Kirwan. Curtis Trowbridge. Even Taffy Sinclair," Jana said. "But Laura McCall and two of her friends were in there, too. THEN, when the bell rang for first period, I couldn't find my schedule card. I thought I'd die! I knew I had English next, but where? I was still flipping through my notebook as I ran out into the hall and almost barreled into a group of ninth-grade girls. You should have seen the looks I got."

"That's awful. What did you do?" asked Katie.

"I just happened to reach into my skirt pocket, and my schedule card was there. And fortunately, I was heading in the right direction."

"You think you had troubles," said Katie. "I needed to use the restroom between classes."

"Yipes!" said Jana.

"I was lucky, though," said Katie. "I found one right outside the cafeteria."

Jana and Katie laughed together, but when Jana looked down the table at Beth, her best friend was gazing off into the distance as if her thoughts were a million miles away.

Jana tried to think of something to say to Beth, something that would get her to open up and tell them what was wrong or at the very least to join in the conversation. Before she could think of anything, Melanie came running up to the table.

"Guess who's in my biology class?" she gushed. "Shane Arrington, and is he cute! In fact, he's gorgeous. He looks just like River Phoenix."

"*The* Shane Arrington of pet iguana fame?" Katie asked sarcastically.

"Oh, yes," said Melanie, melting down into her seat. "And he's darling. I mean, *killer* darling."

"I thought you were madly in love with Scott Daly," Jana reminded her.

"Oh, I am," Melanie insisted. "But you should see Shane. I don't care if his parents are hippies and he has a pet iguana. He is un-*real*!"

"I know," said Jana. "Christie and I are in his homeroom."

"You rats!" cried Melanie. Then she tried to fake sobbing but started giggling instead.

By this time Christie had joined the group. She sat down beside Beth and pulled a sandwich out of her lunch bag with little more than a shy hello in her friends' direction.

Christie was always quiet, but with Beth so unusually silent, Jana had the distinct feeling that the table was weighted like a teeter-totter. All of the talkative ones were holding down one end and the quiet ones were floating somewhere in space at the other.

"Has anyone decided which activities they're going to join?" asked Jana. "Christie and I are thinking about yearbook, school newspaper, and cheerleading."

"And girls' basketball," added Christie.

"You'd never catch me being a cheerleader," said Katie. "Cheerleading is degrading to women."

"Oh, come on, Katie," said Melanie. "You've said that about beauty contests and modeling. Besides, lots of boys are cheerleaders nowadays."

Katie looked huffy. "Well, you won't catch me being one, anyway. I want to do something worthwhile. I'm thinking of running for student council."

Jana groaned and turned to Beth. "Are you going out for the drama club?" she asked.

Beth looked at Jana for a moment. Jana had the feeling from her blank expression that this was the first time she had even considered it. Then she shrugged and picked up her milk carton, draining it as if to say that the subject was closed.

"Well, I heard some more rumors about Laura McCall and her obnoxious friends," said Katie. "The girl sitting next to me in history is from their school. She said that Laura McCall is definitely the leader, just as you heard, Melanie. She also told me something about the other three."

Katie paused, then seeing that she had everyone's attention, she went on. "The little one with the short dark hair is Tammy Lucero. Tammy is cute and bubbly, according to my informant, but she's a terrible gossip. Not only that, but she broadcasts everything she knows to the entire world. Most kids at her other school would have liked her a lot better if she had ever just shut up once in a while."

"Uh-oh," said Jana. "I thought she looked like trouble."

Katie nodded. "The other blonde is Melissa McConnell. Supposedly she's a perfectionist with a capital *P.* You know, straight A's and all that. It seems she looks down her nose at anyone who isn't a perfectionist, too."

"Big deal!" said Melanie, making a face.

"The fourth one is Funny Hawthorne," said Katie.

"FUNNY Hawthorne?" shrieked Jana. "What kind of name is that?"

"It's one of those nicknames that stuck," said Katie. "Her real name is Karen, but everybody calls her Funny, including teachers. Anyway, apparently she's a real bubblehead. She laughs at everything, no matter what happens or what anyone says to her, and she never takes anything seriously. She sounds weird to me."

Jana pulled out her notebook and began writing down the information Katie had just given them. Tammy Lucero, gossip. Melissa McConnell, perfectionist. Funny Hawthorne, bubblehead. She glanced at the list for a moment and then added, Laura McCall, wicked witch.

"Did she say what kinds of things Laura makes them do to stay in the club?" asked Melanie. "I'm dying to find out."

Katie shook her head. "She didn't know. She said they keep it a big secret."

It didn't take long for Jana and her friends to finish their lunches and leave the cafeteria. As they headed down the hall toward the door to the school ground, Jana stopped beside the door marked Girls.

"You guys go on," she called. "I'll be there in a minute."

The others nodded, and Jana pushed through the door into the almost deserted restroom. The door had scarcely closed behind her when she heard it open again and someone come in.

"Thank goodness I caught up with you. I think this is your schedule card. I saw it fall out of your notebook when you left the cafeteria."

Jana spun around. The girl standing there had long, wavy hair and wide blue eyes and such a warm smile that Jana couldn't help returning it.

"Wow. Thanks," said Jana. "That makes twice I've lost it so far today."

"You, too?" said the smiling girl. "I lost mine on the school ground before I even got into the building and a second time in the hall. All I could think about was what if I had to ask a ninth-grader for directions." The girl was laughing now. It was soft, tinkling laughter, and Jana liked the friendly way it sounded.

"That's exactly what happened to me." Jana couldn't believe how much they had in common. "Except instead of before school, I lost my card after homeroom. And now this. *Eeek!* I wonder if I'll survive the day."

"That's the same thing I worried about, so I decided I'd better do something," said the girl. "I taped it inside the cover of my notebook."

"Why didn't I think of that?" said Jana, slapping her forehead with the heel of her hand. "I should have done it before I even left home this morning."

"Here, use my tape," the girl offered cheerfully. As she opened a zipper pocket in her notebook and rummaged through it, Jana studied her face. She was the friendliest person Jana had met all day, and definitely someone she would like to get to know better. At the same time Jana was sure she had seen her before. But before she could make a connection, the girl thrust a roll of tape toward her.

"I always carry this for emergencies," she said, laughing again. "In fact, I carry a lot of things for emergencies. I seem to have a talent for getting into crazy situations."

"Me, *too,*" said Jana, rolling her eyes for emphasis. "I'm the world's biggest klutz."

"Oh, yeah? You think that's bad? I'm a walking disaster. Have you seen the old *I Love Lucy* reruns on TV?"

Jana nodded.

"Well"—the girl moved closer and lowered her voice to confidential tones—"don't tell anybody, but Lucy used to hide out in my bedroom closet. Where do you think she got all her material? From watching me!"

The two girls erupted into giggles. In fact, Jana was laughing so hard that she had trouble taping the schedule inside her notebook. The girl reached out, steadying the notebook for her, and their eyes met for an instant.

"It's super of you to let me use this," Jana said. "I mean that. I'm really grateful." Then, as the girl flashed one last smile and turned to leave, Jana called, "By the way, my name is Jana Morgan. What's yours?"

The girl looked at her questioningly for an instant, and Jana had the feeling that she recognized her, too. Did they know each other from somewhere?

"On my birth certificate it says Karen Janelle Hawthorne," the girl answered almost shyly. "But everybody calls me Funny."

CHAPTER

The two girls parted company with more smiles and with promises to get together soon, but Jana knew that the look on her face must have given away her surprise. Now Jana remembered where she had seen Funny before. At the fence—with Laura McCall. So this was Funny Hawthorne? she mused. Member of The Fantastic Foursome? *Bubblehead?* If those things were true, then why did she seem so nice?

As Jana hurried outside to find her friends, she considered telling them about her encounter with Funny. But she was confused about Funny and wasn't ready to talk about her to anyone yet. Funny was friendly and nice and seemed to be the kind of person Jana would like to know better, but she was a member of The Fantastic Foursome. That could spell trouble.

Glancing around, she saw a group of girls from Mark Twain Elementary gathered near the gum tree. Her four best friends were among them, and so were Alexis Duvall, Sara Sawyer, Lisa Snow, and even Taffy Sinclair. Jana joined them just in time to hear Taffy saying, "Isn't this gross? I mean all that chewing gum. I wouldn't touch it for anything. Just think of how many mouths all of it has been in."

"I think it looks sort of neat," said Sara Sawyer. "If you don't have to touch it, that is."

Jana looked at the tree. Since it was just the first day of school, there were only twenty or so pieces of gum stuck to the bark, but the globs of pink, green, orange, blue, and yellow gave the tree a festive look. Most pieces were just stuck there, as if the chewer had been in a hurry to get inside before the last bell rang. But one piece caught Jana's eye. It had been attached to the main trunk and then stretched out in a long string that had been wound into an artistic design and draped on the tree to look something like a modern art painting.

"I wonder who cleaned off all the old gum from last year?" asked Sara.

"Probably the custodian," said Alexis.

"No!" said Lisa, shaking her head earnestly. "I heard that the seventh-graders have to do it. That's what a girl in my history class says, and she ought to know. She was in seventh grade last year."

"Gross!" said Sara.

"Don't be silly," said Taffy. "She was just putting you on. And even if she wasn't, there's no way *anyone* is going to make me clean somebody else's germy old chewing gum off of this tree!"

Jana shook her head, laughing softly, and glanced up to see Beth sitting alone on the front steps, looking as if she had just lost her last friend. She was holding a small string of beads that was about the size of a child's bracelet in one hand and was rapidly fingering the beads with the other.

Most of the other girls were drifting off in small groups or had disappeared completely as Jana approached Beth. "Hi," she said softly.

"Hi," Beth mumbled without looking up.

"What's wrong?" asked Jana as she sank down to sit on the step beside her friend. "Did you have another fight with Laura McCall?"

Beth didn't answer. Instead she closed the hand that held the beads and slid her left foot forward, concentrating on a spot on the toe of her sneaker.

"You know you can tell me," Jana insisted, scooting closer to Beth. "What is it? Did I do something? Are you mad at me?"

Beth sighed deeply. For a moment Jana thought that she was going to answer. Then without warning Beth jumped to her feet and raced into the building, leaving Jana staring after her feeling both hurt and surprised.

What was wrong with her? Jana thought back over the past few days. She had seemed her old self on Saturday when they had their meeting of The Fabulous Five in her bedroom. It had been Beth who had contributed all the rumors about Laura McCall and her club. Beth had even been the one to suggest that they find a spot by the Wakeman fence just like the one at Mark Twain. What had happened between then and now? Something. Something BIG.

But try as she might, Jana couldn't make a connection between anything she had said or done that could have upset Beth and put her into this black mood. They had talked on the phone a couple of times over the holiday weekend, mostly about what to wear the first day of school, but no cross words had been spoken then. It was as if an invisible curtain had fallen between them.

Jana thought of all the times she had confided in Beth. She had told Beth about her crush on Randy Kirwan before he even noticed her and then about their first kiss. Then there were the times she had told Beth about how she had tried to make contact with her father since her parents' divorce. About her uncertainties regarding her mother's plans to remarry. She had talked to Beth about everything, everything that was important to her, and now Beth had a problem and was shutting her out.

"Come on, Jana! He's over there! Hurry up!" Melanie was breathless and she was tugging at Jana's arm, trying to pull her to her feet. Katie stood beside her. "It's River Phoenix—I mean, Shane Arrington. Come ON, Jana! I'm going to talk to him before I lose my nerve, but I need you and Katie for moral support."

Jana let her worries about Beth slip away as she laughingly got to her feet. "Okay. Okay," she said as she got on one side of Melanie. From the other side Katie looked over at Jana, crossed her eyes, and then silently formed the word "wacko" with her lips. Jana giggled softly and nodded.

Shane Arrington was standing alone by the front door. As they got near him Melanie clutched Jana's arm so tightly that she almost cut off the circulation. Melanie stopped to take a last, deep breath and then started talking.

"You're Shane Arrington, aren't you?" she asked tentatively.

Shane nodded. "Sure am. Who are you?"

"Melanie Edwards," she said, smiling self-consciously, "and these are my friends Jana Morgan and Katie Shannon. We're from Mark Twain. I . . . uh . . . wanted to ask you something."

Shane waited, unblinking, for her to ask her question.

"Is it true that you have a pet iguana named Igor?"

An amused smile crossed his face. "Sure."

"Well, where do you keep him?" asked Melanie. "In a cage?"

"Naw, he has the run of the house."

Melanie's eyes got big and she looked questioningly at first Jana and then Katie. When neither of them said a word, she turned back to Shane.

"But what about when he wants to . . . you know?"

"Go to the bathroom?" Shane asked matter-of-factly. "That's easy. First, he waddles over to the door, and then he knocks on it with his tail. I let him out, and when he wants back in, he knocks on the door with his tail again."

"Oh," said Melanie, and Jana could tell that she wasn't sure whether to believe him or not. "Well. I was just wondering. Thanks a lot."

Shane flashed her a gorgeous smile as the three of them turned and walked away. As soon as they were out of earshot, Melanie stopped.

"Do you think Shane was serious?" she asked. "I mean, could he really train an iguana to go to the door and knock on it with his tail when he wants out?"

"Get real," said Katie. "If lizards could be trained, you'd know it. They'd be performing on Johnny Carson or doing stupid pet tricks on David Letterman."

Melanie didn't look convinced, and Jana had to pinch herself to keep from giggling as the bell rang and Shane disappeared in the crowd pushing in the front door.

"You'd better watch it," Jana warned. "Scott will get jealous."

"Oh, I know," said Melanie. "I really do still like Scott. But you saw Shane. I get weak in the knees just looking at him. Oh, well. I probably don't stand a chance with him anyway."

The girls parted at a juncture in the hallway and headed for their separate classrooms. Jana didn't see Beth all afternoon, but she was surprised to find that Funny Hawthorne was in two of her classes—algebra and history—and that she really did ask her teachers to call her Funny instead of Karen. The name fits, Jana thought. She wanted to start another conversation with her new friend. Funny was like a breath of fresh air after Beth's unexplainable gloom. Instead, she exchanged shy smiles with Funny, putting off anything more until she had time to think it over.

Whitney Larkin was in her algebra class, also. Jana jumped in surprise when Mr. Stone, the algebra teacher, called Whitney's name during roll. Jana looked over at her. Katie had known what she was talking about. Whitney Larkin looked like a pygmy sitting among the other seventh-graders. Jana squinted and studied her closer. She even looked like a genius. Glasses. Serious expression. The works. She would probably show up everybody by raising her hand all the time.

The day finally ended. Jana headed for her locker with mixed feelings about her first day at Wacko Junior High. In some ways it had been awful. Laura and her friends stealing their spot by the fence. Being looked over by a group of ninth-grade boys and only being rated a *three*. Losing her schedule card not once, but twice. And of course, Beth's acting so weird. Still, meeting Funny had made a difference, and so had Randy's 1,000-watt smile in homeroom. Maybe the day hadn't been a total disaster, after all.

CHAPTER

"So how was your first day at Wacko Junior High?" asked Jana's mother when she got home from work later that afternoon.

Jana looked up in surprise from the kitchen table where she was having a snack and doing her homework.

"Awful, mostly, but how did you know we call it Wacko instead of Wakeman? I thought only kids knew that."

"Mothers know everything," Mrs. Morgan teased. "We have eyes in the back of our heads. Ears under our armpits. *Noses between our toeses!*"

"Mom! Cut it out!" Jana cried, but at the same time she was doubled over, laughing. She loved it when her mother clowned around like this. It didn't happen often. Pat Morgan had been divorced from Jana's father since Jana was three, and she had a tough time supporting them on what she made as classified ad manager at the local newspaper. Jana's father was supposed to contribute monthly support checks, but he was an alcoholic, and the checks rarely arrived.

Her mother reached out and smoothed her hair. Then she said, "I'm sorry your first day in junior high was awful. Anything you'd care to talk about?"

Jana shrugged. "It was just the usual stuff. I lost my schedule card—twice. There were a bunch of obnoxious ninth-grade boys looking over the new seventh-grade girls and rating them on a scale of one to ten. Things like that."

Mrs. Morgan looked at her sympathetically. "It will get better, honey. I promise."

Jana closed her book, set her empty plate and glass in the sink, and went to her room. She had purposely left out the part about Laura McCall and The Fantastic Foursome. She didn't want to admit, even to her mother, that she and her friends had practically had a fight with a club from another school or that Laura and her friends were watching every move The Fabulous Five made. But most of all, she had left out two important things: Beth's strange behavior and her instant liking for Funny Hawthorne. She knew what her mother would say. Things were always so simple for grown-ups. She would say that there were only two things to do: call Beth and talk to her, and invite Funny to be friends. But how could she do either of them? She had too much pride to call Beth after the way Beth had refused to talk and then run away, and if she invited Funny Hawthorne to be friends, her other friends, *her best friends forever and ever,* would think she was a traitor.

A little while later her mother called her to the phone. On the other end was Melanie, and she was breathless, as usual.

"I just got back from going to the mall with my mom, so I couldn't call you sooner," she began the instant Jana said hello. "You'll never guess what I walked in on as I was leaving school. When I passed Laura McCall's locker, she was talking to that girl named Funny, except, get this, they weren't talking. They were fighting!"

A mental picture flashed into Jana's mind. She could see Laura's face screwed up into a terrible scowl. It was easy to picture her fighting, but try as she might, Jana simply could not see Funny arguing with anybody.

"Anyway," Melanie went on, "the minute they saw me they shut up and just sort of watched me until I got past them. I don't have any idea what they were saying, but you can believe one thing, Laura McCall was madder than anything. I certainly would hate to have been Funny Hawthorne."

They talked for a few more minutes, mostly about school and what they were going to wear the next day, and then hung up. Had Laura seen Funny and Jana together at noon and figured out that they were getting friendly? She couldn't have, Jana reasoned. Their whole conversation had taken place in the girls' bathroom. But maybe Funny had slipped and said something about Jana, something that set off Laura's temper. Maybe Laura was threatening to kick Funny out of their club if she ever talked to Jana again. Jana shook her head. That was ridiculous. She knew that she was just reading things into what Melanie had said. Probably Laura and Funny were fighting over something that had nothing whatsoever to do with her. Still, she couldn't get the worry out of her mind.

The next morning Jana and her friends met in their special corner of the school ground again. The Fantastic Foursome were nowhere in sight, but nobody seemed to notice. All anyone wanted to talk about was student activities.

"I'm still trying to decide about cheerleading," said Jana. "I wish one of you would try out with me. I'm dying to do it, but I don't want to go by myself. What about you, Christie? You said you might."

Christie shrugged. "I probably won't have time. I'm definitely going out for girls' basketball, and maybe yearbook."

"I wonder what Shane Arrington is going out for?" asked Melanie. "I mean, that's even better than being in a class with him. If we're both in the same activity, we can spend *tons* of time together, and the more he gets to know me, the more he'll see that we're meant for each other."

"Can't you see it all?" asked Katie. "Shane, Melanie, and sweet little Igor. A perfect family."

Everybody broke up over that—even Melanie.

"Well, I don't know about cheerleading yet, but I'm definitely going out for the yearbook," said Jana. "It's called *The Wigwam*, and I've been dying to be on the staff for ages."

"That really is a good idea," said Katie. "I think we should all join the staff together."

"I wonder what kinds of jobs seventh-graders can get?" asked Christie. "Probably all the really good ones are grabbed by eighth- and ninth-graders."

Nobody said anything for a minute until Katie brightened. "Hey, wait a minute. For one thing, I'll bet there's a seventh-grade editor."

"But that's only one job," Jana reminded her.

"So? If there's one good job, maybe there are more," said Katie. "What about reporters and photographers? They must need all sorts of people. We'll just have to wait and find out when we get to the first meeting next week."

"Don't anybody breathe a word to *anybody* that we're signing up for the yearbook," cautioned Christie. "If Laura and her friends find out, you know they'll sign up, too."

When the bell rang, the girls headed for homeroom. Randy was already there, and when he saw Jana, he gave her a little wave that made her heart flip-flop. Jana and Christie kept their eyes on Laura and her friends as much as they were able to during the short homeroom period. Jana had the feeling that they were being watched, too.

After homeroom, when Jana got to her English class, she was surprised to see Funny already seated. She hadn't noticed her in the class the day before, but that was probably because it hadn't been until lunch period that they got acquainted.

"Hi, Jana," called Funny. Then she motioned Jana toward her. "I've saved you a seat."

Funny pointed to the desk next to her own and then removed the notebook she had left there to save the seat. Funny had a huge smile on her face, and Jana couldn't help smiling back as she slid into the seat. Whatever Funny and Laura had been fighting about at the lockers yesterday, Funny didn't seem to be bothered about it now.

"Thanks," Jana said. "I didn't realize you were in this class. Maybe it isn't going to be so dull, after all."

Before Funny could reply, Miss Dickinson came sweeping into the room. Rumor had it that this was Miss Dickinson's first job out of college, and Jana suspected that if dramatics were taught at Wakeman, she would be teaching that instead of English. Her long brown hair was swept up in an old-fashioned pouf with a tiny bun sitting on top like a crown. Her clothes were old-fashioned, too. Today she was wearing an ankle-length blue skirt and a lacy cream-colored blouse with a cameo brooch at her throat.

Jana giggled as she remembered how Miss Dickinson had introduced herself to the class the day before. "My name is Miss Dickinson and I teach English literature and poetry," she had tittered, "but I'm no relation to Emily."

Nobody in the class had gotten it, and she had patiently explained that Emily Dickinson had been a famous poet.

Now as she turned her back on the class and began scribbling on the board, Funny tossed a note onto Jana's desk.

> *Isn't she a riot? It's going to be fun to have a nut for a teacher!!!*
>
> *Funny*

Jana read the note and then nodded to Funny. She glanced up to see that Miss Dickinson was still writing on the board and scribbled an answer on the bottom of the note.

> *Do you think Lucy ever hid out in her bedroom closet?*
>
> *Jana*

Funny covered her mouth with both hands to hide her laughter when she read Jana's note. Then she hurriedly wrote a third message and tossed it back to Jana.

No. It was probably the Three Stooges, instead.
Funny

By this time Miss Dickinson had turned around and instructed the class to open their books. Jana tried to keep her mind on the lesson, but her thoughts kept returning to Funny and the crazy series of notes. She really was a lot of fun. She could even turn a boring old English class into a good time. If only I could become real friends with her, Jana thought. If only my other friends would understand.

Glancing down, Jana saw another note on her desk. She looked questioningly at Funny, who nodded. Jana opened the note, expecting it to be another silly observation about Miss Dickinson. But she was wrong.

Dear Jana,

Are you going to sign up for the yearbook staff? I am. I can't wait. If you sign up, too, maybe they would let us be seventh-grade coeditors. Wouldn't that be a ball?

Please say you'll sign up. Please! Please!

Your new friend,
Funny

Oh, no! thought Jana, and then she clamped her hand over her mouth hoping with all her might that she had not said the words out loud. What would her friends in The Fabulous Five think if she went out for coeditor of the yearbook with one of The Fantastic Foursome? What would her new friend think if she turned her down? What was she going to do?

CHAPTER

7

Jana passed a note back to Funny saying that she hadn't made up her mind yet which activities she would sign up for and that they could talk about it later. That wasn't quite the truth, but at least it would give her some time to think. Her friends in The Fabulous Five would be furious if they found out she was even thinking of trying for coeditor of *The Wigmam* with a member of The Fantastic Foursome. On top of that, Christie had sworn everyone to secrecy about joining the staff.

In the hall between classes, she saw Christie and they walked along together. "Has Beth been acting funny to you?" Christie asked. She had a worried look on her face.

Jana nodded. "She wouldn't even talk to me yesterday. I've been trying to figure out if I've done something to make her mad."

"Same here," said Christie. "She hasn't said two words to any of us since that big blow-up with The Fantastic Foursome at the fence yesterday. I was wondering if there's more to that situation than we realize."

"Do you mean that maybe she and Laura McCall already have some kind of war going on that we don't even know about?"

Christie nodded. "Maybe they met over the summer at the beach or something, and Beth just never told anybody."

"I never thought about anything like that." Jana mulled it over for a moment and then shook her head. "I guess it's possible, but we saw a lot of Beth this summer, and she didn't mention anything about Laura."

"So maybe it was something that was too embarrassing to tell anyone about. Or maybe Laura is blackmailing her. Things like that happen, you know."

Jana shot Christie a quick glance. She was referring to the time in sixth grade when Taffy Sinclair had blackmailed Jana over finding their teacher's wallet after it had been stolen from the classroom. Jana had been innocent, but she had looked guilty, and Taffy had made the most of it.

"Maybe," said Jana, but she still had doubts. Beth was her very best friend. Surely she would have confided in Jana about something like that. Or would she? Beth was changing. There was no doubt about it. Maybe the truth was that she had decided she wanted new friends now that she was in junior high. Maybe she was tired of Jana and the others. Jana shuddered. Maybe, now that they were at Wakeman, nothing would ever be the same.

At lunch everyone was still talking about the latest rumor about Laura McCall. Christie had heard that Laura was planning one of her famous *unchaperoned* parties in the next couple of weeks and that she was planning to invite *all* of the boys from Mark Twain Elementary but *none* of the girls. Everyone was talking about it, that is, except for Beth, who sat at the far end of the table nibbling at her sandwich and ignoring the others. Jana glanced at her from time to time, but Beth seemed to be totally absorbed in her own thoughts. Even her clothes were less flashy than usual, Jana thought. Her slacks and matching shirt were in soft, muted shades of plum.

"I heard that Laura has this big crush on Shane Arrington, but he won't pay any attention to her," said Katie. "She has the parties so she can invite him over and flirt with him."

"Then why is she inviting all the boys from our school?" demanded Jana. "Is she trying to make Shane jealous, or is she looking for someone new to have a crush on?"

Melanie gasped. "That rat! She had better leave Scott alone, and Shane Arrington is definitely too good for her."

"And you know that her three friends are just as bad as she is," said Christie. "I mean, they wouldn't be her *friends* if they weren't."

"Don't any of them have boyfriends from their own school?" asked Melanie. "I mean, there are tons of cute seventh-grade boys from Riverfield."

"From what I hear none of them has a real boyfriend," said Katie. "Melissa McConnell is supposed to have a crush on Jon Smith. You know, the boy whose parents are on television, but she's the only other one of The Fantastic Foursome that I've heard anything about."

"I'll bet that all four of them want to steal Mark Twain boys just to spite us," said Melanie. "What a bunch of jerks!"

Jana's mind was racing. What if Laura picked Randy to go after next? She just might do it, too. She glanced at her friends. They hated Laura McCall, but they didn't like the other three much better, including Funny Hawthorne. She could guess what they would say if she told them that she and Funny were becoming friends.

Suddenly she noticed that Beth was no longer at the table. "Hey, did anyone see where Beth went?" she asked.

Katie shook her head. "What's the matter with her, anyway? She's been acting strange ever since school started. I get the feeling that she doesn't really want to be friends with us anymore."

"You're telling me," said Melanie. "I tried to talk to her this morning, and she almost bit my head off. Do you know what her problem is, Jana?"

"No, but I have to find out." Jana jumped up from the table and crammed the garbage from her lunch back into her paper bag, scooping everything up and heading for the door. "See you guys later," she called back over her shoulder.

She dumped her trash into the plastic can beside the door and dashed into the hall. Beth was nowhere to be seen. I have to find her, Jana told herself. Something's wrong, and I've got to get her to tell me what it is.

The hall was crowded with kids rushing in both directions. She didn't see anybody that she knew well enough to ask if they had seen Beth. Maybe she's in the girls' room, Jana thought. Ducking inside, she looked around quickly, but there was no sign of Beth. Could she have gone outside? Jana wondered.

She had just stepped into the sunlight when she heard someone call her name. It was Funny. She was alone, and she was motioning to Jana. Jana glanced around to make sure none of her friends had come outside. She wasn't sure what they would think if they saw her talking to Funny Hawthorne.

"Listen. It's about Laura," Funny said as soon as Jana got to her. "Don't worry about her. I know you and your friends don't like her. I also know she comes off a little snotty sometimes, but she's really okay. She has a tough time at home with just her dad. He makes her do everything. You know, cook, clean, stuff like that. She says he's never heard of women's liberation. We are always telling her how we'd like to trade places with her and not have a mother hassling us all the time, but she says it's really the pits."

Jana felt as if Funny had read her mind and knew that she and her friends had just been talking about Laura.

"Sure . . . well, okay," Jana floundered. "See you later."

"Okay, but think about what I said about trying for seventh-grade coeditors of the yearbook and call me," Funny insisted. "Here's my number. I wrote it down for you."

What am I getting myself into? Jana wondered as she stuffed Funny's phone number into her pocket and headed across the school ground to look for Beth. Was Funny telling the truth about Laura or just making excuses? After all that Jana had heard about Laura, it was hard to imagine that she needed sympathy for living alone with her father and getting to do practically anything she wanted. She was used to having things her way—at home, with her club, at Riverfield school, and now she was trying to take control at Wakeman Junior High. Not only that, wouldn't Laura be mad at Funny for being friends with Jana the same as Jana's friends would be mad at her?

Just then Jana spotted Beth. She was all alone and she was standing in their special spot gazing out through the chain link fence. Jana stopped. She wanted to run up to Beth and start talking to her and make her understand that whatever the problem was, her best friend was ready to listen. Still, she didn't want to blow it, so she hesitated, stopping a little distance away to plan her next move. Beth hadn't noticed her yet, and as Jana got closer she could see wet streaks on her cheek.

"She's *crying*," Jana whispered to herself. Beth was leaning against the fence and sobbing softly. In one hand was the same small bead bracelet that Jana had seen her holding the day before.

"Beth, what's wrong?" Jana cried, rushing forward. "You can tell me. Honest, you can."

Startled, Beth turned toward Jana, dropping the beads on the ground. The surprise that registered in her eyes for an instant changed to anger.

"Go away!" she shouted. "Just mind your own business and leave me alone!" In one quick motion she scooped up the fallen bracelet and spun away, turning her back on her best friend.

Jana rocked backwards onto her heels as if she had been hit by a tidal wave. She stared at Beth's back, trying to comprehend her words. *Go away. Mind your own business. Leave me alone.* It was clear that their friendship was over.

So, Jana thought, if that's how she wants it, it's all right with me. If she thinks she's too good for her old friends, that's her problem. She stiffened, raised her chin defiantly, and called back, "Okay. Have it your way. I'll leave you alone—FOREVER!"

Then she stomped off in the direction from which she had come, praying silently that Beth had not noticed that there were tears on her cheeks, too.

CHAPTER

8

Jana tried to force herself not to think about Beth all through her afternoon classes. She knew that once she allowed the memory back into her mind, the pain would be almost too much to bear. But she could not keep pictures of Beth—clowning, talking, being a friend—from flashing into her thoughts. Each time that happened she made herself concentrate on Funny. Silly, crazy, *funny* Funny. How super to have a friend like that, one who could make you smile instead of feel like crying, she reminded herself over and over again.

Funny was waiting for Jana in the hall after algebra, and as usual, she was smiling. "Let's walk to history together," she said as she fell in step.

"Sure." Jana returned the smile. Up ahead she could see someone who looked like Beth moving in the same direction as they were going. At least the hair was the same as Beth's. Jana was glad to have someone to talk to, something else to think about.

"Did you ever see so many gorgeous guys under one roof in your entire life?" asked Funny as they stopped outside the door to their history class. "I mean, Copper Beach has a few cute boys, but you girls from Mark Twain Elementary don't know how lucky you are. Your class is filled with hunks!"

"You think *we're* lucky," Jana countered. "Riverfield guys aren't so bad, either. I've seen Shane Arrington. Talk about a hunk!"

Funny giggled. "I'm tired of all those boys. I've known most of them since first grade. Besides, I like your hunks better."

"So which ones did you have in mind?"

"Well . . . there's one named Randy something-or-other that knocks me out. He's got dark, wavy hair—"

"Whoa!" cried Jana. "He's not only taken, he's mine." She smiled and said the words in a teasing way, but she couldn't help feeling a little uneasy, just the same. "Who else do you have your eye on?"

Funny laughed in her usual good-natured way. "Don't worry. I won't go after your boyfriend." Then she gazed off in the distance for an instant as if visualizing one good-looking boy after another and then said, "We-e-e-e-ell, there's a really cute guy named Scott and a gorgeous blonde named Keith. Are they taken, too?"

Jana nodded. "By two of my best friends. Scott is Melanie's boyfriend and Keith is Beth's."

At the mention of Beth, Jana felt a catch in her throat. She had momentarily forgotten about the awful scene at the fence, but Funny was smiling so brightly that she was able to push the memory out of her mind again.

"I promise not to go after Randy," Funny teased, "but I'm not so sure about the other two. Maybe you'd better fill me in on Melanie and Beth so I can analyze my competition."

"Sorry," said Jana. "My lips are sealed."

"Oh, come on. Surely you can tell me one or two juicy little tidbits." Funny's eyes were twinkling and she was rubbing her hands together in delicious anticipation. "Nothing major, of course. Just something itsy-bitsy that I can use against them."

I love this, Jana thought. It's so much fun to joke with Funny. Aloud, she said, "Nope. You could tickle me with a thousand feathers, and I wouldn't breathe a word. You could . . ."

Suddenly Jana's face froze in the middle of a smile. She had the creepy feeling that someone was looking at her. Glancing around quickly, she found herself staring straight into Katie Shannon's eyes. Beside her stood Christie, and she was looking at Jana, too. Neither of them was smiling, and Jana knew instantly why. It was because she was talking to Funny. After all, Funny was one of The Fantastic Foursome, one of Laura's followers. *The enemy.*

Jana shrugged and gave them an apologetic smile as she ducked into the classroom. "Come on, Funny, we'll have to talk later," she mumbled. "We'd better go in now. It's almost time for the bell."

Once she slid into her seat, Jana glanced back at the door. She couldn't see Christie and Katie anymore. She was glad. Part of her felt guilty for talking to Funny and for enjoying it so much, but another part of her was angry. It was obvious what they had been thinking, but they had misunderstood. Funny was a super person, nothing like Laura McCall. How could they be so blind?

Jana sighed. She couldn't remember when she had felt so depressed. During lunch period she had lost her best friend for no reason at all except that she had wanted to help. Now two of her other friends were being unreasonable because she was talking to someone else. But Jana didn't realize just how unreasonable until she went to her locker after school and found Christie, Katie, and Melanie waiting for her.

"What's going on between you and Funny Hawthorne?" Katie challenged before Jana could even get her locker door open. "Every time I look around I see the two of you talking together."

"And laughing," added Christie. "Don't you like your old friends anymore?"

"First Beth deserts The Fabulous Five and now you," added Melanie.

Jana was stunned. "Hey, you guys. Hold on a minute. Since when is it a crime to talk to somebody outside The Fabulous Five?"

"It's not a crime," Christie insisted. "It's just that we get the feeling that you'd rather be with her than us, which is really strange since she's one of *them*."

"Right," said Katie. "After all of the things we've heard about The Fantastic Foursome."

"So, did it ever occur to you that some of those rumors might not be true? Besides, what have you heard about Funny Hawthorne? That she's a bubblehead? Well, let me tell you, she's just a nice person. That's all. She happens to have a great sense of humor. I suppose that makes her a bubblehead, right? If that's the case, I'd be happy if people called me a bubblehead, too."

Spinning around, Jana stomped off, leaving her bewildered friends staring after her.

CHAPTER

"They think I'm a traitor," Jana complained at the dinner table. She had just finished telling her mother about the terrible scene at her locker after school. "They think I'm being disloyal to them—my old friends—just because I've made a new friend. It isn't fair. No. It's worse than that. It's STUPID."

Mrs. Morgan was quiet for a moment, studying the swirls in her coffee as she slowly stirred it. "It sounds to me as if they're worried."

"Why would they be worried?" asked Jana.

"They think that you don't like them anymore. Maybe they just need reassuring. Did you tell them that nothing has changed the way you feel about them?"

"Of course not," Jana snapped. "I don't have to tell them a thing like that. They *know.* Besides, why wouldn't I like them now just as much as always?"

Her mother shrugged. "You've got me," she said, smiling sympathetically. "It never hurts to remind people of how you feel about them, though."

"If you ask me, they ought to trust me. I mean, we've been friends forever. I shouldn't have to go around saying, 'I really like you! I really like you!' like some kind of broken record."

Her mother didn't answer. Jana was silent for the rest of the meal, too. It didn't make sense that her friends would think she didn't like them anymore. They were just jealous. And that didn't make sense, either, after all the years they had been friends. But it was true.

That still didn't explain Beth, Jana thought with a sigh. She hadn't told her mother about that yet. What was the use, anyway? Her mom would say what grown-ups always said, talk to her and work things out. How could she talk to Beth when Beth wouldn't talk back?

The phone rang, jolting Jana out of her thoughts.

"It's for you," her mother said. Then she put her hand over the mouthpiece and added with a smile, "This call might just make things a little better."

"Hi."

Jana felt like melting down into her shoes at the sound of Randy Kirwan's voice. "Hi, back," she said softly.

"How is school going?" he asked. "Did you get any good teachers?"

"Besides Mr. Neal, I got Miss Dickinson for English. She looks as if she's going to be fun. How about you?"

"No. Nobody special. I'm more interested in football. With the Mark Twain guys and some of the Riverfield and Copper Beach guys going out, we ought to have a good team."

Jana had an instant vision of Randy's scoring a touchdown with the crowd cheering, just the same way it used to happen at Mark Twain Elementary.

"Are you going to the movie and then to Bumpers Friday night?" he asked. "It should be a lot of fun."

"Probably," she said, and then crossed her fingers behind her back. "I haven't asked Mom yet, though."

"Scott and Mark and I talked about going. I hope you go. I'll see you there if you do."

Jana thought she heard his voice get softer when he said that, and it made her feel good all over. They talked a little while longer, and when they hung up, Jana decided that her mother had been right. That telephone call *had* made things better.

In her room a little while later, Jana thought again about what her mother had said about her friends. Maybe she should call Katie and Christie and

Melanie. Not to reassure them, as her mother had suggested, but to find out what was wrong with them. She could call them one at a time and ask them why they were acting so . . . so . . . so *stupid.* She hated to use that word, but it seemed to be the only one that fit.

"Stupid. Stupid. Stupid," she whispered over and over again, but instead of the anger she expected to feel, helpless tears flashed into her eyes.

A little while later she heard the phone ring again, and then her mother's voice called out, "Jana, it's for you."

Rats! she thought. The truth of the matter was that she didn't want to talk to anyone. Not Katie. Not Christie. Not Melanie. She thought about pretending to be asleep, but she knew her mother would never let her get away with that. Dragging herself away from her desk, Jana went to the phone and barely mumbled hello.

"It's me, Funny," came a bubbly voice. "Is everything okay?"

Jana stared at the phone in surprise. "Sure," she lied. "Everything's fine. Why?"

"It's just that I noticed the look you got from your two friends when we were standing in the hall before history class. And then I was near the front door when you came barreling out after school. You were all by yourself and you looked furious. I just thought maybe something was wrong."

Jana didn't answer. It wasn't her so-called *friends* calling, the ones who were causing her problems. No, it was Funny. Kind, caring Funny—her new friend.

"I'll bet I'm the problem," Funny added shyly.

"Well . . . sort of," Jana confessed. "They think I'm a traitor for being friends with you."

"Believe me, I understand. Laura has been giving me a hard time about you, too. She keeps saying things like, 'You seem to be forgetting who your real friends are. We've stuck together through thick and thin.' Things like that."

"And what's so ridiculous is that they're really super friends," Jana went on. "I just don't understand what's wrong with them."

Funny sighed deeply. "Well, I don't want to come between you and your friends. The other thing I called to say was that you don't have to try for seventh-grade coeditor of the yearbook with me at the sign-up meeting next week if you'd rather not. I'll understand."

"I want to!" Jana practically shouted the words into the phone, surprising herself at the feeling of determination that was swelling within her. "Nobody is going to tell me who to be friends with." Then she added in a softer voice, "But you don't have to, either, if it's going to make your friends mad."

"I think my friends should understand," said Funny, "and if they don't understand, they're not my friends."

"You're right. What we really ought to do is meet and walk to school together in the morning. When they see that they can't intimidate us, maybe they'll leave us alone and let us be friends."

"Do you want to?" asked Funny.

"Sure. Do you?"

"Okay," said Funny. "Where shall we meet?"

Jana thought a minute. It should be a few blocks from school. A place where they could meet without many kids seeing them so that they could pull their act together before making a grand entrance on the school ground. Maybe even the same place she and the rest of The Fabulous Five had met on the first morning of school. "Do you know the corner by Nugent's grocery?"

"Sure."

"Great. Be there at eight-thirty, and we'll march onto the school ground together and really give our friends something to talk about."

The girls talked for a little while longer. After they hung up and Jana was back in her room, she couldn't help wondering if she had done the right thing. What if it backfired? What if she lost her old friends and things didn't work out with Funny? Where would she be then?

She drummed her fingertips on her desk and thought again about calling Christie, Katie, and Melanie. Maybe they really were so insecure that they needed to hear that she still liked them. But did she? After the way they were treating her? she asked herself. It was a puzzle that didn't seem to have an answer.

Sliding into bed, she reached over and turned Randy's picture so that she could see him better. She smiled at him before she turned off the lamp and drifted off to sleep.

CHAPTER

10

Funny was bouncing up and down in eager anticipation, and she began waving wildly when she saw Jana headed her way the next morning.

"Wow! I don't know why I'm so nervous," said Funny. "I had an awful time getting to sleep last night. I just kept thinking about what everyone will say when they see us coming to school together."

Jana smiled weakly. "Me, too," she admitted.

"You don't want to chicken out, do you?"

"No," said Jana. "Not unless you do."

Funny squared her shoulders. "Nope," she said defiantly. "I've made up my mind, so let's go."

Jana looked at her new friend with admiration. Funny definitely wasn't a bubblehead.

When they walked onto the school ground, Jana had the crazy feeling that she had just stepped into the center of a stage. It seemed as if everyone stopped to look at the two of them. Even kids they didn't know.

"This is weird," she whispered.

"It's probably just our imagination," said Funny.

Jana nodded, but she could see the other members of The Fabulous Five standing by the fence staring as if they were seeing ghosts. Near the front door, Laura and the rest of The Fantastic Foursome were staring, too. So were Alexis Duvall, Sara Sawyer, and Lisa Snow, who were clustered on the sidewalk.

"Say something funny," Jana ordered. "Then we'll laugh like crazy, make a mad dash for the building, and duck inside."

"Oh, sure," said Funny. "Just like that, I'm supposed to turn into a comedian."

"Okay, tell me about Shane Arrington. I heard that he has a pet iguana."

This time Funny actually did burst out laughing. "Oh, so you've heard about Igor?"

Jana faked a big laugh and looked straight at Funny so that she wouldn't have to meet anyone else's eyes. "Yeah, Igor!" she cried. "Isn't he hysterical?"

Funny caught on to the trick, and the two of them ignored everyone and giggled wildly as they headed into the building, collapsing against the water fountain once they were safely inside and out of sight of the others.

Now Funny was giggling for real. "Wasn't that a blast? And did you catch the looks on everybody's faces when they saw us together?"

"Did I ever? I guess we showed them."

Things were great, Jana thought, so long as Funny and she could stick together. They knew people were watching them whisper and talk as if they had been best friends for ages. It was fun, but Jana's nervousness returned when the first bell rang and she made her way through the crowded halls toward homeroom. Laura McCall was in that homeroom, and so were her friends Tammy Lucero and Melissa McConnell. That was bad enough, but so was one of her own best friends, Christie Winchell.

Jana got there first and scrunched down into her seat, wishing she could become invisible. As much as she wanted to show her friends that she had a right to be independent and make other friends, the thought of any of them being truly angry with her was awful. *What should I do when Christie comes into the room?* Jana wondered. *Should I look up and say hi as if nothing has happened? Or should I wait for her to say something to me first?* What a choice, Jana thought. *If I look up first, it will give her the perfect opportunity to snub me. But if I don't look up, she'll think I'm snubbing her.*

If only Randy would come in now, she thought. *If only he would stop at my desk, give me one of* his 1,000-watt smiles and say "Hi, Jana" in his gorgeous, masculine voice.

"Hi, Jana," said a masculine voice.

Hopeful, she glanced up into a smiling face. The only trouble was, it belonged to Curtis Trowbridge.

"Hi, Curtis," she mumbled, and thought, Rats! Why did it have to be him? Then, in a flash of inspiration, her face brightened and she added, "So what do you think of Wacko Junior High?"

It wasn't that she really cared what Curtis thought about anything, but if she could involve herself in a conversation with someone, even nerd-of-the-world Curtis, then she wouldn't have to make the first move when Christie came in. How could she speak to Christie if she was busy talking to Curtis?

Curtis's smile stretched wider, and he literally leapt down the aisle and landed beside her desk. "It's terrific! I like all my classes and every single one of my teachers."

Jana groaned inwardly. Nobody but Curtis would go around shouting about how much he liked his classes and his teachers. She forced herself to smile at him and say, "That's great, Curtis. That's really great."

Glancing around Curtis, she saw that Christie had just sat down at her desk. There was an angry look on her face that made Jana cringe.

Suddenly Curtis's voice cut into her thoughts. "Well, are you?" he was insisting.

"Oh, sorry, Curtis," Jana stammered. "I missed that question. What did you want to know?"

"If you're going to join the newspaper staff." There was an exasperated sound in his voice.

Before she could answer him, the bell rang, and Mr. Neal motioned everyone to their seats and began taking roll. Jana breathed a sigh of relief. Her plan had worked. She had avoided having to look at Christie. Out of the corner of her eye she could see that Christie was staring straight ahead. The stony expression was still on her face.

Jana looked away. Maybe she had been wrong to avoid speaking to Christie. Now Christie probably thought it was Jana who didn't want to speak. She started to sneak another look at Christie when she realized that Christie was looking at her. *Eek!* thought Jana. What should I do now?

Taking a deep breath, she turned her head slowly toward her friend. She would look at Christie, maybe even smile, and see what happened. But Christie turned her head abruptly, looking away from Jana before their eyes could meet.

Now what? thought Jana. Maybe if I stare at her, she'll have to look back. I'll even give her a big smile to show her that if there's a problem between us, it's all her fault.

Jana answered when her name was called and then took a deep breath, slowly swinging her eyes around toward Christie. Christie fidgeted slightly, and a spot of color appeared on her cheek, but she continued to stare straight ahead. She knows I'm looking at her, Jana thought. *Why doesn't she look back?*

Snapping her eyes forward again, Jana opened her notebook. She would die before she would let Christie make a fool out of her. Grabbing her pencil, she began doodling. Anything to look busy, she thought. I don't have time for stuck-up friends.

When the bell rang ending homeroom, Christie was the first one out of her seat and through the door. It was only then that Jana looked down to see what she had doodled all over the page:

T-R-A-I-T-O-R

CHAPTER

11

Jana stayed glued to her seat while the rest of the class filed out of homeroom. She was staring at the doodles on the page.

T-R-A-I-T-O-R T-R-A-I-T-O-R
T-R-A-I-T-O-R

I'm not a traitor, she thought stubbornly, but still, it was pretty obvious that her friends saw her that way.

She made it to English class just as the bell was ringing. Fortunately Funny had saved her a seat, and she sank into it just as Miss Dickinson was announcing the assignment. She gave Funny a quick smile and opened her book. Deep down she was glad that there wasn't time for conversation with Funny. As much as she liked her new friend, a lump the size of a tennis ball formed in her throat every time she thought about Melanie, Christie, Katie, and especially Beth. She couldn't just abandon them completely and spend all of her time with Funny. It wasn't the same. Something was missing. There were no memories of things they had done together the way there were with her old friends. With The Fabulous Five she had memories of good times. Even of bad times. Hadn't Laura reminded Funny that they had stuck together through thick and thin? She had been talking about the very same thing, only Jana hadn't realized what she meant until Christie had refused to look at her in homeroom.

Thick and thin, she mused, thinking of all their problems with Taffy Sinclair. The club they'd had against Taffy. The time she got a part on a soap opera. The time she blackmailed Jana! Her friends had stuck by her and helped her out of every one of those dilemmas. They had helped her in her romance with Randy Kirwan, too. Wonderful Randy, who was not only the handsomest boy in the world but the kindest and most sincere, also. She thought about his call last night. What would he think of her if he suspected that she was abandoning her best friends? The thought hit her like a bolt of lightning. She couldn't lose Randy Kirwan. She just couldn't.

Morning classes went on as usual, but Jana hardly noticed what was going on. Her mind was on her friends in The Fabulous Five and the misunderstanding that was growing between them. Maybe Mom was right, she thought. Even though they should know that they were special to her without being told, if they needed reassuring, she would do it. At lunch period, she thought. I'll do it then. It was amazing how easy it would be now that she thought about it. She would simply march up to their table and say that she had something to talk about. Then she would explain how much she still wanted to be friends with them. Surely they would listen, and when they did, everything would be all right again. She would explain about Funny, too. About how she was a nice person, not a bubblehead, and how they ought to give her a chance.

Jana was actually humming to herself as she got her lunch out of her locker and headed for the cafeteria. Her plan was going to work. She was sure it would. She forced herself to hang back a little, letting the lunchroom fill up so that her friends would be sure to be there when she went in. She giggled to herself, feeling a little like Taffy Sinclair making a grand entrance. That's okay, she told herself. It's for a *fabulous* cause.

She had barely stepped inside the cafeteria when she heard a familiar voice call her name.

"Jana! Jana! Over here," Funny gushed. She was sitting at a table not three feet from the door and she was waving like mad. "Hurry. I've had a terrible time holding your seat."

Jana's heart sank. There was no way she could ignore Funny without insulting her. Scanning the cafeteria, she saw her friends sitting at a table on the opposite side of the room. How could she ever get over there to talk to them?

Just then a brilliant idea struck. "Milk," she called back to Funny. "I've got to get in line for milk. I'll come back as soon as I can."

"I got your milk," cried Funny. "See!" She was holding up two cartons, one in each hand, and grinning like mad. "Sit down."

Jana sighed and joined Funny at the table. She tried to smile and mumble thanks, but her heart felt as if it were made of lead and her appetite was totally gone. She couldn't talk to her friends with Funny around. She had to get to them *alone.* But how?

"What's wrong?" Funny asked around a bite of apple. "Bad morning?"

Jana nodded, glad to have an excuse for her behavior. She didn't want to hurt Funny. After all, it wasn't Funny's fault that she had gotten herself into such a mess.

"Me, too," Funny confessed. "Talk about freeze out. Of course, Laura's the worst, but whatever she does, Tammy and Melissa do also."

"I've heard some things about Laura," said Jana.

"Like what?"

"That she's in control of your group, and if she tells you to do something and you won't do it, you're out. Is that true?"

Funny shrugged. "I've heard some things about The Fabulous Five, too," she said, and Jana had the distinct feeling that she was changing the subject to keep from talking about Laura. "For instance, is it true that your club used to be *against* Taffy Sinclair?"

Jana frowned. It hurt to hear The Fabulous Five being criticized. "Taffy's not so bad *now*," she said. "But she used to be the snottiest person alive. You just don't know her."

"You don't know Laura, either," countered Funny. Then her face brightened. "Hey, let's not get into an argument. If we lose each other, we're *doomed*!" Then she put one hand around her neck, stuck out her tongue, and made a strangling sound, which sent Jana into convulsions of laughter in spite of herself.

Jana didn't get a chance to talk to her friends anytime during lunch period. Funny Hawthorne stuck to her like frost, giggling and chattering as if things could not be better. To make matters worse, Jana saw Katie and Christie on the way to history class, but when she waved to them and tried to motion with her hands for them to wait for her, they wheeled around and stomped off in the opposite direction.

"What am I going to do?" she said half aloud as she opened her history book. "I've got to talk to them, but how?"

After school, she thought. After school I'll call an emergency meeting of The Fabulous Five. Why didn't I think of it before? While her history teacher droned on about the winning of the American West, Jana was busy writing notes. She wrote one to Christie. One to Katie. One to Melanie. And one to Beth. Maybe Beth wouldn't come, but she had to try.

Emergency meeting of The Fabulous Five at my house after school. This is urgent. BE THERE!!!

Jana

Between classes Jana raced to the hall where the seventh-grade lockers were and slipped a rolled-up note into the U-shaped shank of the combination lock on each door. They can't open their lockers without finding them, she thought happily. And they'll come. I know they will. And when I explain to them about how I feel, everything will be all right again.

Still, she couldn't resist crossing and uncrossing her fingers three times for luck.

CHAPTER

12

Jana couldn't remember when she had been so nervous. She hadn't even stopped by her locker after school. Partly it was because she didn't want to come face-to-face with her friends when they found her notes, but mostly it was because she was in a hurry to get home and get ready for the meeting.

She tore around the apartment straightening up, plumping pillows on the sofa, checking the refrigerator for soda, and doing a million and one things that she didn't ordinarily bother to do when her friends were coming over. But this meeting was important, she told herself, and special.

When the doorbell rang, she almost jumped out of her skin. Putting her hand on the knob, she took a deep breath to steady herself and opened the door. It was Melanie.

"Hi," she said weakly.

"Hi," said Jana. "Come on in."

"Can I use your phone to call my mom and tell her where I am?" asked Melanie.

Jana nodded. She was glad that Melanie wanted to use the phone. Maybe the others would get there before she was forced to make conversation. Things were so awkward now, and she wanted everyone present before she made the speech she had been rehearsing in her head all afternoon.

The doorbell rang again. It was Christie and Katie. They peered anxiously into the apartment when she answered the door but seemed to relax when they saw that Melanie was already there.

Jana busied herself in the kitchen fixing drinks while the others got settled. She knew she was stalling as she checked each glass for smudges, counted out exactly four ice cubes per glass, and poured the soda very slowly so that it wouldn't bubble over the top, but she was getting more panicky by the minute. Should she start explaining as soon as she passed out the sodas? But Beth wasn't there. What if she didn't show up? How long should she wait?

Three pairs of eyes met her as she entered the room, carrying the sodas.

"So what's the emergency?" asked Katie in a cool voice.

"Yeah, you said it was urgent," said Christie.

Even though Beth hadn't arrived, Jana knew she couldn't stall any longer, so she set the glasses on the coffee table where everyone could reach them and began.

"There is an emergency. A BIG one. Probably the biggest one we've ever had. There's something none of you seem to know, and if you don't find out right now, something awful is going to happen to The Fabulous Five."

Melanie gasped. "What are you talking about?"

"I'll bet I know," said Katie. "Rumors! I'll bet Laura McCall is spreading rumors about us again." She shot a warning glance at Jana and added, "It better not be anything you told that Funny Hawthorne."

Jana bristled. "It has nothing to do with rumors," she insisted. "And I have not told Funny anything about The Fabulous Five. What I'm trying to tell you is, I'm not a traitor. I like Funny Hawthorne. She's nice and we're starting to be friends. But you are my very best friends in the world, and I really, *really* don't want that to change . . . because if it changes, we won't be The Fabulous Five anymore . . . and I don't think I could stand that."

Nobody said anything for a moment. Jana could feel all their eyes on her, but she couldn't look at them. Her heart was too full of pain, and tears were brimming in her eyes and threatening to spill down her cheeks. What if they didn't believe her? What if they didn't *care*?

Suddenly Melanie sprang off the sofa and threw her arms around Jana. She didn't even notice that she had nudged the coffee table, rocking it so that the glasses teetered and then tumbled over, spraying the room and everyone in it with soda and ice cubes.

"Oh, Jana," she cried. "We want to stay friends! We really do!"

They were all crying now, and Christie and Katie rushed over and wrapped their arms around her, too.

"It was awful without you," said Christie. "We *weren't* The Fabulous Five."

"Nothing was the same," insisted Katie. "Honest, but we thought you didn't like us anymore. We thought that when you got to Wakeman and met Funny and started spending all that time with her that suddenly we weren't good enough for you anymore."

"That's not it at all!" Jana protested. "It is true that I made a new friend, but nobody could ever take your place, and as far as spending more time with her than you, she's in more of my classes than any of you are."

A moment later everyone was crawling around the floor, blotting wet spots, picking up ice cubes, and talking at once.

"We really missed you," said Melanie. "I was so upset that I couldn't even think about Scott or Shane. All I could think about was you."

"Yeah," added Katie with a grin. "And when Melanie can't think about *boys*, you know she has problems."

"Okay, guys," said Jana. "I feel a lot better now that you understand. I also hope you'll give Funny a chance. She's not like Laura. Believe me. She's not a bubblehead, either. She's just got a great sense of humor."

The others shrugged, and Jana could see that they weren't totally sold on Funny. I'll drop it for now, she thought. At least I've made a little progress. And the best thing of all, The Fabulous Five are back together!

Jana stopped and looked at her friends. "The Fabulous FIVE," she whispered. "Where's Beth?"

"Who knows?" muttered Katie. "She hasn't spoken to any of us for a couple of days."

"She acts as if she's far off somewhere," said Christie.

"*So* far off that she even has her own zip code," Melanie said wryly.

Frowning, Jana said, "I thought it was just me she was mad at. I mean, really mad, and I don't know what I've done." She explained to them about the scene at the fence and Beth's angry insistence that she be left alone. "I've never seen her like that," said Jana. "It was unreal."

"One thing's certain," said Christie. "It isn't just you she's mad at. And have you been noticing that bracelet she carries all the time?"

"It looks like a child's bracelet," added Melanie.

"Yes," said Jana. "She had it on the school steps and again at the fence. I'd never seen it before that. Have you?"

No one had.

"I'm really worried," said Jana. "Maybe she isn't mad. *Maybe* she's in some sort of trouble."

"And needs us," whispered Melanie, her eyes growing wide.

Jana raced to the phone and punched in Beth's number. "She always goes straight home after school unless she's coming over here," she reasoned.

She held the receiver away from her ear so that all four of them could count the rings. Finally, after fifteen, she hung up the phone. Before everyone left, they tried again—this time they let it ring twenty times—and Jana tried twice before she went to bed, but still, there was no answer.

CHAPTER

13

Beth was not at school the next day. Jana met Christie, Melanie, and Katie at their spot by the fence before classes, and although they waited until the very last minute to go into the building, she didn't show up.

"I tried to call her again before I went to bed last night," said Jana as they turned into the corridor where the seventh-graders had their lockers.

"So did I," said Christie. "Nobody answered. What's going on, anyway?"

"At first I thought she might have a cold or the flu or something like that," said Katie. "But then she would be at home to answer the phone."

"Or at least one of her parents would answer," added Melanie. "Did anyone call her this morning?"

No one had, and Jana was sorry that she hadn't thought of it herself. "Let's meet at noon and call her from the phone in the office," she suggested. "There's probably some simple explanation, and we'll all feel a lot better when we find out what it is."

Everyone agreed and went off to their homerooms. Jana scarcely heard what was going on in hers. All she could think about was Beth and the strange way she had been acting ever since the first day of school. Even her looks were different. Instead of the bright, kooky outfits she usually wore, she had dressed in dark colors and wore no jewelry for almost the whole week. No chunky necklaces. No long dangling earrings. No jewelry at all except for the bead bracelet she carried in her hand and played with all the time. Did it have something to do with her problem? A child's bead bracelet? But what? It didn't make any sense.

When she got to English class, Funny was her usual bubbly self. "Can you believe it? It's Friday. TGIF. Isn't that great?"

Jana nodded. She couldn't help smiling at Funny, and Funny went right on talking before Jana could get a word in edgewise.

"Tonight's movie night, too. Isn't it exciting? We'll really feel like we're in junior high instead of grade school after the movie and Bumpers. Are you going with Randy?"

"No. I'll see him there, though. He called me the night before last and said he'll be there with Scott and Mark and some of the other guys."

"How about Keith?" asked Funny. "Do you think he's going?"

"He wouldn't miss it." Then Jana laughed and added, "Hey, why all the questions about those guys? I thought you weren't going to get interested in Keith OR Scott OR Randy? Remember? You promised since they're taken."

"I know they're taken," said Funny, sounding a little miffed by Jana's insinuation. "But they're still cute, and just because I asked if they're going to the movie tonight doesn't mean I'm going to do anything."

"Sorry. I guess I'm a little touchy right now." Jana went on to tell Funny about Beth and how worried she and her friends were. "It's really weird that someone in her family isn't answering her phone."

"Maybe they had to go out of town for something," offered Funny.

"Maybe. But if it was something like that, surely she would have told someone."

By lunchtime Jana was more worried than ever. She had exhausted every possible excuse she could think of, and nothing sounded reasonable.

The four girls went straight to the office when the lunch bell rang. No one was interested in eating until they had tried once more to reach Beth. This time Melanie punched in the number, but it didn't change anything. The phone rang and rang without anyone's picking up on the other end.

"I just don't understand it," said Jana, shaking her head.

She was deep in thought when they headed for the cafeteria and was surprised when she heard Katie say, "Get a load of who has our guys cornered. Of all the nerve!"

Jana snapped to attention and focused on a group of boys and girls just ahead in the hall. Randy was there, and Scott and Keith, but that wasn't all. When she saw who the girls were, a small cry of alarm escaped from Jana's lips. "Funny!" she said barely above a whisper. "And Laura!"

The two members of The Fantastic Foursome had definitely cornered the three boys from Mark Twain Elementary. The five of them seemed to be having a great time talking and laughing.

Every once in a while Jana could catch a word of their conversation. ". . . movie . . . tonight . . . Bumpers . . ." The more she heard, the more her anger grew.

"I don't like this," said Melanie. Turning accusingly to Jana she added, "I thought you said Funny Hawthorne was okay. If that's true, what are she and Laura doing flirting with our guys?"

All Jana could do was shrug. She certainly couldn't defend Funny. What was more, she wasn't sure she wanted to. Especially since Randy was one of the boys she and Laura had been flirting with.

Between algebra and history classes, Jana stopped Funny in the hall.

"I just can't believe it," she said angrily. "After promising to leave our boyfriends alone, you and Laura McCall had the *nerve* to flirt with them in the hall at noon."

Funny started to speak, but Jana cut her off. "Don't deny it," she charged. "I saw you, and so did my friends. And you did it after I talked you up and told them what a great person you are."

Funny's large eyes filled with tears. "I know how it looked," she protested, "but it wasn't that way at all. Laura and I just happened to be walking in the hall and the boys came along. Laura said hi and they said hi, and the next thing we knew we were talking to them. That's all there was to it. Honest."

Jana wanted to believe her, and the look of misery on Funny's face almost convinced her that she had been wrong. But still, something was nagging at her. Something she couldn't quite put a finger on was making her doubt Funny's sincerity.

"Okay," she conceded. "I believe you." It wasn't quite true, but Jana didn't want to start any more arguments until she had time to think things through.

Funny's face lit up as if it were the sun just emerging from behind a dark cloud. "I knew you'd understand," she gushed. "I'll see you tonight at the movie and at Bumpers afterward. Okay? Everybody's going to be there. It's going to be a blast."

It wasn't until the two had parted that Jana realized what had been bothering her about Funny. It was the rumors about Laura McCall's making her friends do things to prove their loyalty and stay in her club. Could it be possible that Funny had only been pretending to be her friend? Had Laura put her up to it? Had she forced Funny to spy on The Fabulous Five and report everything she found out—including information on their boyfriends—to her? Maybe that was what Funny and Laura had been arguing about at the lockers when Melanie overheard them a couple of days ago. Maybe Funny hadn't wanted to spy, but Laura had forced her.

The more Jana thought about it, the more convinced she became. Who would suspect a happy, carefree person such as Funny? A bubblehead? Hadn't Funny followed her into the girls' bathroom the day they met and started the conversation herself? Sure, she had Jana's schedule card, but she might have been just waiting for an opportunity like that. And hadn't Funny been terribly anxious to turn her back on her old friends and make friends with Jana?

It all fit like pieces to a puzzle. Laura and the rest of The Fantastic Foursome were probably laughing their heads off at Jana and The Fabulous Five. And then she remembered the snatches of conversation she had heard when Funny and Laura were talking to the boys in the hall. *Movie . . . tonight . . . Bum-*

pers. The rumors were right. Laura McCall was sending Funny to spy on The Fabulous Five, just as she had suspected, but that was only part of her plan.

CHAPTER

The sidewalk in front of the theater was crowded with kids from Wakeman Junior High when Jana and her three friends arrived half an hour before time for the movie to begin. Jana's spirits rose even though she had still not been able to reach Beth or to resolve her doubts about Funny Hawthorne.

Some boys she didn't know were horsing around, but most kids were either waiting in line to buy tickets or standing around in small groups talking.

"Hey, Jana!" It was Curtis, and he skidded to a stop beside her. He was all smiles as he pushed his glasses up on his nose and waited expectantly for her to answer.

"Hi, Curtis," she said.

"Mark Twain kids are sitting on the left side," he told her. "Do you want me to save some seats?"

Jana shook her head. "Thanks, but I'm not sure how many of us are sitting together. We'll see you inside."

She looked past Curtis and scanned the crowd. Randy and his friends had just gotten their tickets and were going in the door.

"There's Jon Smith standing over there by himself," said Christie. She was pointing toward a boy leaning against the building. "Isn't he cute?"

Jana glanced at him and then smiled at Christie and nodded. Jon Smith was medium height with medium brown hair and a medium build. Nothing great, compared to Randy Kirwan, and he certainly didn't look as if he had celebrities for parents. *But*, she thought as she looked him over for a second time, he wasn't so bad either.

Alexis Duvall and Lisa Snow were in the ticket line and waved when Jana looked their way. There were lots of kids from her old school here. She was relieved that they wouldn't be outnumbered, since it was a Friday night tradition for Mark Twain seventh-graders to sit on one side of the theater and Riverfield seventh-graders to sit on the other.

Finally Jana spotted Laura McCall and her three friends. They had just piled out of a small red sports car that was pulling away from the curb, and they were coming across the street toward the theater with Laura in the lead and the other three trailing behind her. She looked terrific in tight-fitting jeans and a fringed western jacket. It was obvious from the way her eyes darted around that she was looking for someone—someone she intended to impress. Jana had the sinking feeling that she knew who that someone was.

By this time her friends had noticed The Fantastic Foursome also.

"Look out. Here they come," Katie buzzed in Jana's ear.

"Laura had better leave Scott and Shane alone," warned Melanie.

Just then Jana's eyes met Funny's. Jana wanted to look away, but Funny gazed at her with such a pleading expression that she couldn't. Jana raised her hand in a brief wave and allowed a smile to flicker across her face. Then she led her friends toward the ticket line before Funny could respond.

It was World War Three inside the theater. The two schools were squared off at each other over a chasm of empty seats in the middle. Straw papers whizzed overhead like miniature rockets, and every couple of minutes bomb blasts sounded as someone else stamped on a popcorn box. Ushers stormed up and down the aisles shushing some kids, warning others, and generally having no effect at all.

Jana couldn't help smiling to herself as she clutched popcorn in one hand and a Coke in the other and hurried down the aisle. Just as she saw

Randy several rows ahead, she felt someone pinch her arm.

"Over there!" Melanie whispered excitedly. She had seen the boys, too, and was urging everyone in that direction.

"Great," said Jana. "There are four seats right behind Randy and Scott. Let's grab them before someone else gets them." Silently she was feeling superior. Laura McCall would have to sit on the other side of the theater. Randy, Scott, and Keith were safe from her clutches—at least for now.

"Hi, Jana Banana," shouted Joel Murphy just as Jana slid into a seat.

Jana hated that nickname, and she started to scowl and shout something back at him when Randy turned around and gave her one of his 1,000-watt smiles. Her heart turned at least a dozen flip-flops as she sank deeper into her seat and returned his smile.

"Hi," he said. "You're still going to Bumpers after the show, right?"

All she could do was nod.

"Great," he said, smiling again. "I'll see you there, and I'll walk you home."

Jana didn't see any of the movie. She was too busy daydreaming about Randy and making up stories about what would happen when they got to Bumpers. Laura would be there, too, of course, trying desperately to get Randy's attention. But he wouldn't notice her. He would be gazing into Jana's eyes, telling her how wonderful she was while Laura could only watch and sob her heart out. Then later, he would walk her home, and maybe he would kiss her again. She hugged herself at the thought.

A couple of times Jana noticed Laura and Melissa McConnell strolling up the aisle on the Mark Twain side. Laura pretended to look straight ahead, as if she just *happened* to be on the Mark Twain side of the theater, but Jana knew better. She could see them looking for Randy and Mark and Keith out of the corners of their eyes. Ha! thought Jana. Are they ever going to be in for a big surprise when we get to Bumpers.

When the movie ended, everyone tried to stuff themselves through the exit at once. It took forever to get out, and Jana could see that a big crowd had already made it to Bumpers ahead of them. She had never been inside the fast food restaurant before since it was strictly a junior high school hangout, but she had heard a lot about it. It was called Bumpers because it was decorated with bumper cars and posters from an amusement park ride. Some cars were hanging from the ceiling by wires. Others were arranged around the room for kids to sit in. The old bumper cars were freshly painted in reds, greens, yellows, and blues, but they still had dents and bashed-in fenders from their days of careening around and smashing into each other.

"Wow! This place is neat," cried Jana over the noisy crowd. "But where on earth are we going to sit?"

"The boys have a big booth over there," Christie shouted. She was pointing toward a booth near the counter.

Jana craned her neck to see who was sitting there. It was Randy, Scott, Mark, Joel, and Keith. "Come on," she said, and motioned the others to follow her. "There's room for all of us."

They tried to push through the crowd, stopping once to let a waiter carrying a tray loaded with burgers and fries pass in front of them.

"This is a worse madhouse than the theater," complained Katie.

Finally a path opened up, but just as Jana started to make a break for Randy's booth, she stopped cold and stared. Laura McCall and her friends were heading in the same direction. The only trouble was, they were in the lead, reaching the booth and pushing their way in before Jana and her friends could get there.

"What are we going to do?" Melanie wailed in Jana's ear. "*They've* got *our* seats!"

Just then Laura caught sight of Jana. She narrowed her eyes and flicked her long braid from side to side, looking like a cat about to attack its prey.

Jana could hear someone shouting in the background, but she was too angry to pay attention. She couldn't let The Fantastic Foursome get away with this. She had to do something. But what?

"Jana Morgan!" a man's voice shouted. "There is a telephone call for Jana Morgan!"

Jana spun around and looked toward the counter where a man in a cook's apron was holding a telephone receiver above his head. Had she heard right? she wondered. Had he called her name?

"JANA MORGAN!" he repeated. "Is there a Jana Morgan in here?"

"Here!" she shouted, jumping up and down and waving her hands over her head. It was for her, but who could be calling her at Bumpers? Kids parted, making a path for her as she raced to the man. "I'm Jana Morgan," she panted.

"Hello?" she shouted, putting the receiver to one ear and a hand over the other ear to shut out some of the noise.

"Hi, honey. It's your mom. I'm sorry to interrupt your fun, but have you seen Beth anywhere tonight?"

"Beth?" she asked in alarm. "No! She wasn't at school today, either, and nobody answers her phone. But how did you know? What's wrong?"

"I just had a call from her father. He said she's disappeared, and he hoped she was with you. According to Mr. Barry, Beth's mother underwent surgery today. Didn't you know about that, either?"

"No, Mom. What's wrong with her?"

"She had a lump in her breast and they thought it might be cancer, but *thank goodness*, the tests were negative."

"At least that much is a relief," said Jana, "but it explains a lot, too. Beth's been acting awfully strange for the past few days. In fact, she wouldn't speak to any of us. We thought she was mad about something. We didn't know she was worried about her mother. But what happened to Beth? What do you mean, she disappeared?"

"Beth and her father were in the hospital lounge a few hours ago waiting for word that Mrs. Barry had come through surgery okay. He thinks Beth dropped off to sleep and woke up just as the doctor was giving bad news to someone else waiting in the same lounge. Beth must have been so groggy from her nap that she thought the bad news was about her mother because she jumped up, raced out the door, and he hasn't been able to find her since."

"That's awful!" cried Jana.

"Poor Beth," said Mrs. Morgan. "There's no telling where she's gone or what she's going through right now."

Jana promised her mother that she would find out if anyone at Bumpers had seen Beth or had any ideas where she might have gone, and then she would come right home. As she put down the receiver, tears flashed into her eyes. *Poor Beth*, her mother had said. *There's no telling where she's gone or what she's going through right now.*

I've let her down, Jana thought miserably. Why didn't I make her tell me what was wrong? Why didn't I try harder to find her? She's my very best friend in the world, and when she needed me, I let her down.

CHAPTER 15

Taking a deep breath, Jana turned and faced the crowd. Everyone was talking and laughing as if it were the greatest night in the world. Waving her hands over her head, she tried to get their attention. Nobody looked or paid the slightest bit of attention to her. Tears spurted into her eyes. She had to find out if anyone had seen Beth or had any clues to where she might be. Quickly she scrambled up onto the counter, astounding the man in the cook's apron and everyone else nearby. "Quiet, please!" she shouted. "This is an emergency! May I have everyone's attention?"

Slowly a hush spread over the crowd as Jana continued to call for silence. Finally, every eye in

Bumpers was on her. She cleared her throat, wiped the tears from her eyes, and said, "I just found out that Beth Barry is missing."

Her words were met with gasps and murmurs from shocked boys and girls in the crowd, but they quieted down again immediately and leaned closer to hear as she explained about Mrs. Barry's surgery and the misunderstanding that had caused Beth to run away.

"Everybody think hard. This is important. Has anybody seen her anywhere today or this evening?"

Heads shook and kids talked quietly among themselves, but no one came forward with information about Beth. Katie, Melanie, and Christie stood close by, looking as stricken at the news as Jana felt. They helped her jump down from the counter and briefly described Beth to the man in the cook's apron, who introduced himself as Mr. Matson and said he was the owner of Bumpers and wanted to help.

"What are we going to do?" she sobbed as kids drifted out the door and headed for home.

Just then an arm slipped around her shoulder. "It'll be okay," said Randy, gently pushing her head onto his shoulder. "We'll find her."

Later, he walked her home just as he had promised, but instead of kissing, they made plans for what they would do if Beth wasn't home by morning.

Jana stared at the ceiling all night long worrying about her best friend and trying to figure out where she might be. She and Randy had hurried home, hoping that by then her mother had heard good news, but she hadn't. Poor Beth, Jana thought. She believed her mother had died. Jana wanted so badly to find her and tell her that her fears were wrong.

Early the next morning Jana and her mom called Mr. Barry, but there was still no good news about Beth. Then she called Randy to put their plan into action.

Splashing cold water on her face and jumping into her most comfortable jeans and sweatshirt, Jana was gulping down a glass of orange juice when the phone rang.

"Oh, my gosh!" she shouted. She dashed past her mother and lunged for it, nearly dropping the receiver in her excitement. "HELLO!"

"Hi, Jana. It's me, Funny. I just called to see if Beth has been found yet."

"Not yet." Jana collapsed limply onto the sofa, feeling breath leave her lungs like air rushing out of a balloon. "I was hoping that you were Mr. Barry . . . or Beth."

"I'm really sorry," said Funny. "I didn't get a chance to tell you last night in all the excitement. Can I come over and wait with you?"

"I won't be here. All the kids from Mark Twain are meeting at the mall when it opens at ten. It was Randy's idea, and he's calling everyone and telling them what to do. We're going to form search teams and comb the whole town looking for her."

"Wow! What a great idea. Can I help?"

"No," snapped Jana. "It will just be Mark Twain kids."

Even though Funny was silent, Jana could tell she was hurt. In some ways Jana was sorry, but Funny would just have to understand. It was something private that they wanted to do together. At least, she wanted it that way. She wanted things the way they used to be, without anyone from Riverfield horning in.

The doors hadn't opened yet when she got to the mall, but already a few kids were standing outside. Marcie Bee, Gloria Drexler, and Sara Sawyer were leaning against the building. Richie Corrierro and Joel Murphy were locking their bikes in a rack by the front door, and Taffy Sinclair and Alexis Duvall were crossing the parking lot. No one smiled or said much of anything. It was as if they were going to a funeral, Jana thought, and then shuddered. She couldn't let herself or them think that way. Her heart was pounding, and the lump in her throat kept growing larger. As frightened as she had been last night when she heard that Beth had disappeared, somehow she had honestly believed that everything would be all right by morning. Things such as this happened to other people. You read about it in the paper all the time. But it never happened to her . . . or to *Beth*.

A couple of minutes later a man in a security guard's uniform opened the mall doors. Jana and the others went in, heading for the goldfish pond by the escalators where they had agreed to meet. One by one the others arrived. Christie Winchell. Randy Kirwan. Scott Daly. Lisa Snow. Clarence Marshall. Mark Peters. Curtis Trowbridge. Katie Shannon. Melanie Edwards. Mona Vaughn, and the others, until all twenty-six members of Miss Wiggins's sixth-grade class at Mark Twain Elementary had assembled except one—Beth Barry.

Randy came over to stand beside Jana as she held up her hand for quiet, even though it wasn't necessary. Everyone was already quiet, stunned and silent as they worried about their classmate, and they were looking to her, Beth's best friend, to tell them what to do next.

"First," she said, "has anybody thought of any place she might have gone?"

"Did they search the hospital?" asked Matt Zeboski. "She might have just ducked into an empty room where she could be alone and think."

Jana nodded. "They looked there. In every room and every supply closet and behind every door that she could have opened."

"What about her grandmother or an uncle or cousin or someone like that," offered Kim Baxter.

Jana sighed. "They checked them, too. Doesn't anyone have any *new* ideas?" she blurted, aware that panic was creeping into her voice. "We have to find her! Come on, everybody. Think!"

Just then Jana was aware that more kids were joining their group. She looked up and gasped. "What are you doing here?" she said angrily.

Laura McCall was standing slightly in front of her three friends, but it was Funny Hawthorne who stepped forward and spoke.

"We want to help. Honest. We really do."

"How could you figure out where Beth would go?" challenged Alexis Duvall. "You hardly even know her."

"Yeah," murmured others in the crowd.

"I have an idea," offered Laura. "At least I know where I go when I'm upset." Everyone got quiet and looked at her. "It may sound silly, but I go to my old playhouse in my backyard. When I was little I always went out there and told my troubles to my dolls, probably because it was my favorite spot in the world. My very best memories are there. My dolls aren't there anymore, but I still feel safe and protected there, anyway."

"But Beth doesn't have a . . . playhouse . . ." Jana started to protest, but she stopped in the middle of the sentence, suddenly understanding what Laura was getting at. "You're saying that we should try to figure out where she felt the happiest and most secure because that might be where she is right now."

Laura nodded.

Jana looked at her friends. There was one place that they had all wished they were over and over again during this first wacko week of junior high, she thought. Mark Twain Elementary. Was it possible that Beth had hidden there? Had she taken refuge in the school where she had been so happy in the past now that she thought the future looked so bleak? She could have gotten in yesterday afternoon before the building was locked and hidden out until everyone went home.

A cheer went up when Jana suggested their old school. A lot of kids agreed that it was a logical place to look.

"I'll call my mom and ask her to meet us there with the key," called Christie, running for the pay phones.

"Let's go," shouted Randy. He took Jana's hand and gave it a quick squeeze, and she gave him a smile back that said thank-you. Then he added, "Even if she loves Mark Twain enough to hide there, she's probably pretty scared right now."

"And lonely," added Melanie. "Let's just hope she's there and that she's okay."

Jana started to leave with the others, but instead she stopped and turned to Funny. "I'm sorry I doubted your friendship. Come with us. We want you to." Then, motioning to all of The Fantastic Foursome, she added, "If we find her at Mark Twain, we'll have you to thank, Laura. It really is a good idea."

The entire group marched out of the mall and toward the school together, spilling over the sidewalk and into the street. Some jogged in nervous anticipation. Others pushed bikes. Jana walked along with her arms around two of her friends, Melanie on one side and Funny on the other.

The crowd got quiet as they approached the school. Mrs. Winchell's car stopped at the curb a moment later. Jana and the others milled around anxiously while she found her key. "I hope you kids are right about her being here," she said as the lock turned and the door swung open. "Beth!" she called into the empty corridor. "Beth Barry. Are you here?"

Only silence greeted them, and after a moment they tiptoed inside in single file.

"It sure is spooky in here," whispered Funny.

Jana nodded and looked around. The morning light was slanting in the windows, causing long shadows to angle off eerily. But most of all, somehow Mark Twain Elementary looked smaller than she remembered it after a week at Wakeman Junior High.

"Beth Barry? Are you here?" Mrs. Winchell repeated insistently. This time when no one answered, she added, "Okay, let's fan out in all directions. Be careful, though. She's very upset. We don't want to scare her any more than she already has been."

Jana motioned to Katie, Christie, and Melanie to come with her. "I'll bet I know where she is," she whispered.

When they reached their old sixth-grade classroom the door was closed. All the others along the hall were open. Jana pointed to the door. "She's in there," she said, forming the words by moving her lips and not making a sound. The others nodded that they understood.

Now what can we do? wondered Jana. She agreed with Mrs. Winchell about how upset Beth was. They had to be careful. Suddenly it dawned on her. She knew exactly what to do.

She pressed her face against the door. "Beth," she called softly. "It's Jana. Listen. I have something wonderful to tell you. That doctor you heard in the waiting room wasn't talking to you. Your mother's okay. She came through the operation just fine, and she's going to get well. Please come out now. She wants to see you."

The four friends joined hands and held their breaths. Was Beth really inside? Had she heard what Jana had said? Finally the door opened a crack. From inside came one sniffling sound and then another.

"Beth?" Jana pleaded. "Did you hear what I said? It was all a misunderstanding. Your mother is okay."

This time the door swung open all the way and Beth stepped out. Her eyes were puffy and her hair a tangled mess, but she was smiling.

"Oh, Jana," she cried, rushing into her best friend's arms. "I've been so scared. I thought that she was . . ."

"It's okay," said Melanie, putting her arms around Beth and Jana. Christie and Katie joined in, and the five of them stood in the middle of the hall hugging and crying tears of happiness.

CHAPTER

16

The next day was Sunday, and Jana's mother invited Beth and her father to come over for dinner after they visited Mrs. Barry at the hospital.

Beth was all smiles. She even looked normal again in a bright fuchsia miniskirt and matching knit top and huge, brightly colored earrings in the shape of parrots. "You should see Mom! She's walking up and down the halls, and the doctor said she can go home sometime this week."

"That's terrific," said Mrs. Morgan. "I'm glad that everything worked out so well." She excused the girls right after dessert, saying that she and Jana would do the dishes later.

It was only then, after the girls were in Jana's room with the door closed, that Beth told Jana the rest of the story.

"It's hard to explain," she said, "and I know you think that I get carried away and overly dramatic about things sometimes, but this is true. I was really worried that my mother would die and that it was all my fault."

"Beth!" Jana exclaimed. "How could you believe such a thing?"

Beth gave her friend a helpless shrug. "Believe it or not, it all started when I was five years old. I yelled at Mom. Things like, 'I hate you,' ' I wish you were dead.' The kind of things little kids say without thinking. Later that afternoon Mom was in an automobile accident coming home from the grocery store. I thought she was going to die, and I thought it was all my fault. And then last weekend we had a big fight over new clothes for junior high. Later that night I found out she was going into the hospital for surgery, and—I couldn't help it—the old guilt came back again." She wiped away a tear.

"But your mother didn't die in the accident or in surgery," Jana insisted. "Besides, you don't really believe in superstitions like that anymore. You're old enough to know better."

"I know," confessed Beth, sighing. "But it's happened a couple of other times. Nothing as serious as a car accident or an operation, but I guess it *was* enough to make me superstitious, like you said. I told you it was going to sound weird. That's why I couldn't talk to you about it and why you thought I was mad at you and didn't want to be friends anymore. I was mad at myself for hurting my mom."

"Oh, Beth," cried Jana, throwing her arms around her best friend. "I didn't know what to think. And then you were always playing with that little bracelet. What was that all about?"

Slowly Beth pulled the bracelet out of her pocket and dropped it into Jana's wastebasket. "I guess I won't need this anymore." She grinned sheepishly. "It goes back to Mom's car accident when I was five. There was a lady in the hospital waiting room that time who was holding beads. I was too small to know that they were a rosary and that she was praying, so when she got good news, I decided I would get my beads, too. When I went home that night I got out my bracelet and held it in my hand all night long. The next morning they told us Mom was going to be okay. Even though I knew the bracelet didn't have any magical powers, I just couldn't help it. I got it out again when she went into the hospital. Does that make any sense?"

Jana nodded. She really did understand. It was easy sometimes to believe something even though you knew deep down that it couldn't possibly be true. Poor Beth, she thought. All these years she's been blaming herself for things she had nothing to do with, and her superstitious fears had even made her run away.

"Promise me one thing," she said, taking Beth's hand. "You won't forget that The Fabulous Five always stick together and talk their problems over with each other."

Beth laughed. "I promise," she said. "Now let's decide what we're going to wear to school on Monday."

"Okay," said Jana. "I can't wait to get back to Wacko Junior High!" It surprised Jana to hear herself say that, but the more she thought about it, the more she knew it was true. She had grown up a lot over the past few days, and she was ready to leave Mark Twain Elementary behind and go on to junior high.

Later, after Beth and her father went home, Jana went to the phone and called Funny.

"Hi," said Jana. "I just want you to know how much I appreciate your help in finding Beth. I have to admit that I was wrong, especially about Laura. If she hadn't come up with that idea, we might still be looking for Beth."

Funny laughed a tinkling little laugh. "I told you Laura was okay. She just comes off wrong sometimes."

"Yeah, well, I shouldn't have been so quick to believe the rumors I heard. I should have tried to find out the truth for myself."

"You mean about my being a bubblehead?"

Jana gasped. "You know about that?" she shrieked.

"Sure. I think it's a riot."

Jana couldn't help breaking up over that. All this time she had thought that calling Funny a bubblehead would be a put-down, and Funny, with her usual sense of humor, thought it was . . . *funny*.

"Do you still want to try for coeditors of the yearbook?" Jana asked once they had stopped laughing. "My friends can handle it now. They're still my BEST friends, and I'll go around with them most of the time, but I'd like to be your friend, too."

"I feel the same way," said Funny. "I guess my deepest loyalties are still to Laura and Tammy and Melissa. We've been friends for a long time, but I like you, also."

After they hung up, Jana gave herself a hug. It had been quite a first week at Wacko Junior High. Her friendships and her loyalties had been put to the test. She had found out that you couldn't believe all the rumors you heard, and she had made a new friend without losing her old ones.

In fact, she thought with a grin, the best news of all was that things had never been more fabulous among The Fabulous Five.

CHAPTER

17

Beth was breathless as she raced to the spot by the school fence where The Fabulous Five met every morning before class. "You're not going to believe this," she said, "but the rumor we heard before is true. Laura McCall *is* going to have a party, and—get this!—she's asking everyone from *her* old school, but she's inviting ALL of the boys and NONE of the girls from Mark Twain!"

"Wait a minute," said Jana. "How do you know? It's probably just some rumor The Fantastic Foursome are spreading to make us mad." Even though Laura had come up with the idea that had led them to Beth when she was missing, Jana still wasn't certain they could trust her.

"Lisa Snow said that Laura and her friends are passing out invitations in RED ENVELOPES to the boys," said Beth.

"Red envelopes?" said Katie, making a face. "How corny. Are they supposed to look like valentines or something?"

Beth shrugged. "Who knows? But Lisa found out from Mark Peters. He said that he got one and so did every other seventh-grade boy from Mark Twain. And even worse, they're all planning to go."

"Boy, that's sneaky," said Christie. "Everyone says that her dad lets her do anything she wants to do and that he isn't even home when she has her parties. How could the boys resist going?"

Melanie was fuming. "Laura wants all the boys for herself," she blurted out. "She's been trying to get Shane Arrington for ages, and now she's going after my boyfriend, Scott Daly, too. *Well, she can't have either one of them. I'll make sure of that!*"

Will Laura succeed in having all of the Mark Twain boys and none of the girls at her party? What will Melanie do to keep Laura away from both Shane and Scott? Find out in *The Fabulous Five #2: THE TROUBLE WITH FLIRTING.*

ABOUT THE AUTHOR

Betsy Haynes, the daughter of a former newswoman, began scribbling poetry and short stories as soon as she learned to write. A serious writing career, however, had to wait until after her marriage and the arrival of her two children. But that early practice must have paid off, for within three months Mrs. Haynes had sold her first story. In addition to a number of magazine short stories and The Fabulous Five series, Mrs. Haynes is the author of the Taffy Sinclair series, *The Great Mom Swap*, and its sequel, *The Great Boyfriend Trap*. She lives in Colleyville, Texas, with her husband, who is also an author.